MW01269262

Romeo's Revenge
and other Wisconsin stories

Byron Grush

In memory of Gordon Yadon, historian and author and long-time resident of Delavan, Wisconsin.

CONTENTS

	Author's Introduction	1
1	Romeo's Revenge	3
2	One False Spring	14
3	Erik Takes a Trip	20
4	My Cousin Jeanie	32
5	On the Brule	42
6	Giants in the Earth	53
7	Ghost Story	68
8	Nobody Liked Ludwig	92
9	The Balloon Ascensionist's Wife	103
10	The Lost Prince of Green Bay	128
11	Barnum's Gold	139
12	The Fire Next Time	159
13	Up the Big River from *Once Upon a Gold Rush*	172

INTRODUCTION

These are stories of historical fiction; that is, they are woven into the fine fabric of time as if they had actually happened. Thus I have occasionally used people and events for which there may be historical documentation and I have attempted to treat them fairly and adequately. However, the reader is warned not to believe anything they read between the pages of this book, at least not without doing their own research. That said, I hope you will enjoy these fantasies that I have distilled from my experiences, the life and times of interesting people and places I have come across, and my own meager imagination. Here are a dozen stories based on the State of Wisconsin and its rich history: the elephants, giants, gangsters, lost princes and other unique characters that have roamed this sweet land. As a bonus, the book contains a chapter from my historical novel, *Once Upon a Gold Rush*, with the hopes that the reader will be intrigued.

ROMEO'S REVENGE

Juliette died in the winter of 1864, a winter so harsh that ice crystals filling the air were wind-whipped against exposed skin by the Wisconsin Chinook, biting and stinging like tiny hornets. The ground froze so solid that Juliette could not be buried. Instead, she was set upon the thick ice at the middle of Lake Delavan, there to await the spring thaw. In future, fisherman would bring up her huge bones with stout lines. The task of dragging her body across the ice fell to Romeo. Some say it drove him mad, caused him to kill five men during the course of his melancholic life. Perhaps this was true, but Romeo had plenty of reasons to hate all mankind; circus life was not easy for an elephant.

Juliette wasn't the love of Romeo's life. Romeo's star-crossed romantic attentions went to Canada, another sweet lady elephant that had been acquired by the Mabie Brothers' Circus through the usual route: German hunters stalking the African veldt kill a mother elephant for her ivory, capture the baby, transport it and other wild animals in wooden crates across the desert by camel caravan, travel from Judah to Suez by Turkish steamer, through Greece and Italy back to Germany by rail, where several months later, those animals still living are sold to the highest bidders among the zoos and circuses of Europe and the Americas.

Canada and Romeo shared a boxcar as the Mabie Brothers' Circus train pulled away from the winter quarters in Delavan, Wisconsin, and headed west toward show dates in Nebraska. Romeo was 19½ feet high at the shoulder and weighed over 10,000 pounds. By comparison, Canada was petite, but the combined tonnage of the two pachyderms strained the timbers of the boxcar as it rumbled along an older roadbed in the midst of Iowan cornfields.

Tom Cavendish, one of the animal trainers and the only human Romeo liked, entered the car to check on the elephants. Dry rot in the floorboards gave a spongy feel as he stepped around hay bales to stroke Romeo's swaying trunk.

The train slowed as it approached a trestle. The ravine thirty feet below was nearly dry of water, the spring rains yet a few weeks off. As the engine reached the other side, the engineer was startled to see an obstruction on the tracks ahead. A fallen tree lay across the rails like a drunken sailor. The engineer quickly released the throttle and pulled heavily on the brake lever. The train lunged to a sudden stop. Animals and people in every car were flung forward. Canada fell with an impact that splintered the floor of the car, trapping her in a hole. As she struggled the hole widened, shards of rotted wood tumbling into the ravine below. As Tom Cavendish watched in horror, she began to slip downward. He ran for help.

When Tom and several roustabouts returned moments later carrying coils of rope they witnessed an amazing scene: Romeo stood over Canada, his trunk supporting her entire bulk as she dangled helplessly through the hole that opened onto to a perilous plunge to sharp rocks.

They edged their way around the larger elephant to get closer to Canada, risking being crushed against the boxcar's wall if Romeo shifted position. Tom leaned over the hole and studied the situation. Even if they could loop the rope around Canada's immense body it was doubtful they could pull her up. If the train began to move again she would snag against the trestle and the whole train might fall into the ravine. Romeo was unable to lift her and might be pulled into the abyss as well as more and more of the floor gave way. It became clear that they would save only one elephant that day.

"Romeo, old pal," Tom said softly into the great beast's ear, "it's time to let go of her." Romeo would not budge. He held on although he was slipping slowly toward the orifice in which his bride hung suspended, swinging to and fro like a gigantic pendulum.

"Gene...Roy..." shouted Tom, "the rope! Pull it around Romeo. Quickly!"

The two roustabouts complied and soon Romeo was tethered securely to the metal platform at the entrance to the boxcar. Still the elephant held tight to Canada. The ordeal continued for the better part of an hour while various officials of the circus conferred and Tom stayed by Romeo's side, speaking softly to him. Finally, Romeo's strength gave out and Canada slipped gradually from his grip. She fell into the ravine with a crash that was drowned out by Romeo's wail—a mournful trumpeting that no one who heard it, ever wanted to experience again.

It would be logical to assume that Canada's death was the turning point for Romeo, that from that moment on the human race, all except Tom Cavendish, would become his mortal enemy. Certainly he withdrew into despondency. The elephant's malaise could be read upon his normally stoical countenance like a sad novel.

He refused to perform his dance under the big top a few days later, standing stiff and still like a great grey mountain as the other elephants lifted feet and swung trunks to the calliope's sanguine resonance. He did his work without his usual buoyancy, pulling up stakes and carrying timbers at a sluggish pace. He merely tolerated his drudge persona. He was no longer the first in line to push wagons as he had once been. Thus handlers less able than Tom began to prod and poke and found themselves dodging Romeo's flailing trunk; that huge appendage crashed like a felled ponderosa pine against barn or wagon just where the fleeing handlers had stood.

Romeo had always been a bit of a rascal. Stealing Cookie's cooling pies, burning his tongue, and so chasing Cookie up a tree in revenge—they say an elephant never forgets. He was a proficient escape artist, opening barn doors, unearthing the sturdiest of stakes where he was chained, making off with forty pound bags of grain while still dragging his chain. He often rampaged through the darkened streets at night of whatever town they had camped at, but always returned at dawn before residents could panic at the sight of him, a behemoth, knocking over sheds and fences, scaring dogs and horses. But he hadn't killed anyone—yet.

Jake O'Reilly's death might have been an accident. He shouldn't have been in the elephant tent at night. He surely shouldn't have been drunk. He was wrong to sing an Irish drinking song so loudly, substituting the name, "Romeo" for the villain of the piece. Nor should he have slapped Romeo on the ear in playful jest. The circus hands playing poker in the next tent heard his singing. Then they heard Romeo's trumpeting and Jake's frantic screaming. Then silence. Jake lived for two days, his broken body lying on an old cot in the ringmaster's tent; the clowns, bareback riders, acrobats, tightrope walkers and roustabouts attending to him in vain. His last words were, "Damn that elephant!" There would be more accidents.

If Romeo had lost a love, Tom Cavendish had found one. Rose had been born into a family of equestrians and started riding bareback at the age of four. She, her mother, father and older brother were billed as "The Fabulous Fenton Family," and toured as a featured act in the Mabie Brothers' Circus.

Rose was an expert at the backward flip, a somersault executed from a rear facing stance on a galloping horse, landing, of course, on the horse as it careened around the ring. This dangerous feat was surpassed only by the family's "Flying Pyramid" formed by father and son riding four horses, each straddling a pair, with mother and daughter standing on their shoulders holding American flags. The ending was most dramatic as Rose and her mother simultaneously somersaulted to the horses' rear quarters, then to the sawdust floor of the center ring, all the time waving their flags triumphantly.

Rose Fenton and Tom Cavendish first connected one evening when a cyclone ripped uncomfortably close to the circus encampment near Council Bluffs, a small town across the river from Omaha. Wind and rain battered down the smaller tents. Caged lions flung themselves against wet bars, snarling and roaring in fear and anger. Elephants strained against their chains, trumpeting and stomping their huge feet, bedlam rivaling the thunder.

Men ran through the downpour with large wooden mallets, pounding on tent stakes loosened by the blustering tempest. Rose and Tom huddled together under a wagon which creaked and chattered as the deluge pounded against it. In crisp blue-white lightning flashes Tom looked into green eyes, wide with fear, saw a tender waif, flotsam from the storm, clinging, crying out for comfort, and so drew her to him with strong arms and soft whispers. The long, slow kiss that followed had been inevitable and overdue for they had passed many furtive glances and spoken many trivialities which both knew were the hesitant meanderings of desire restrained by protocol and station. For the one single hindrance to their romance was the fact that Rose was married.

At sixteen Rose had married George Herbert Hershberger, clown magician, and expert knife thrower. Hershberger had approached Rose's parents, promised to provide for her, refused to talk of dowry, and won them over with an insidious charm which masked the lust that actually motivated him. Rose was a natural beauty, thin but muscular, and moved with a fluid grace that beguiled George Hershberger. The vision of her lithe form atop a powerful steed hurtling across the sawdust set him on fire. But his passion was not shared by the young girl. Soon she returned to her parents' lodgings at winter quarters. It was around the time the elephant, Juliette, was put on ice. George watched Rose with jealous vigor, making it known to all that she was his possession and that he would recapture, if not her affection, at least her physical being.

That George Hershberger was a philanderer was well known. In his clown magician act, the lady clown he pretended to saw in half had told tales of his advances toward her. In the world of circus clowns a protective attitude prevailed, especially toward those few women that donned rubber noses. George was confronted by three harlequins in full makeup one night after the show, but as he was over six feet tall and weighed over 250 pounds, the encounter stopped short of fisticuffs. He then turned his attentions toward his assistant in the knife impalement act. Here his seduction succeeded.

The lady in question, Isadora Mobley, whose stage name was Zaza, felt a tingling sensation with each nearly missing blade that outlined her sequined body against the wooden backdrop as if it were near-sexual penetration. She thrilled at the danger, marveled at the accuracy with which George could place each knife so close to her skin that goose pimples formed next to the cold steel. When he propositioned her, she surrendered willingly and with a passion that might have unnerved George, caused his hand to tremble, his aim to waver, had not George been distracted by a young bareback rider named Rose.

When Zaza learned of George's engagement to Rose she was furious. She confronted him in the dressing room where he was applying the elaborate clown face he wore in his magic act. His design, unique as all clown makeup was, was not the traditional happy, comical face with oversized minstrel show style lips and exaggerated lifted eyebrows; instead it featured a down-turned frown and a glistening tear that trailed from an eye crossed vertically by a deep crimson line like a gash. It was a face that scared small children. Zaza stormed into the room, a barrage of venomous insults and rebukes thickening the air. The rhubarb reverberated throughout the encampment.

The tension between the two affected the knife impalement act. Perhaps Zaza flinched. Perhaps George flared in anger for just an instant delaying the release of the knife one one-hundredth of a second too late. Perhaps an ill wind blew through the big top that day. The blade plunged into the backboard with a sharp thunk, removing a one inch piece of flesh from Zaza's left bicep. It was the last performance she would give with the knife thrower.

For the next few weeks, as George was unable to interest anyone in taking Zaza's place, he began to develop a routine involving a very long rawhide bullwhip. He was able to snap a cigarette in half while held in the mouth of a straw dummy, but so far he had not found any human dummy to enlist in the new act. He took to wearing the coiled whip hung from his belt in a sort of warped defiance of propriety. It was an affectation that would lead to tragedy.

Ropes rattled against rippling canvas—canvas which flapped like the wings of startled pigeons where it split open for a doorway into the big tent. Dust devils swirled up loose top soil and torn ticket stubs from the Indiana farmer's field where the circus had set up for a late autumn show. Inside on the bleachers the anticipation and sheer glee of children and parents alike bristled like static electricity along a cat's back. Mothers held tight to babies for fear of dropping them between the hard wooden boards that served as seats. Hawkers threw bags of peanuts to the upper levels and money passed down hand to hand. The clowns were already working the crowd, their slapstick antics delighting those in the front rows. Then a hush fell over the audience as the ring master, splendiferous in red coat and shiny black top hat, strolled to the center of the ring.

"Lay—dees and gentlemen, chill—dren of all ages," he began. They had heard it many times before but they still loved it. "Welcome to the Mabie Brothers' Circus and Menagerie Extravaganza! The show is about to begin!"

A roar of applause arose when curtains parted and the circus performers marched in as the band played "It's a Grand Old Flag." Acrobats leaped and turned cartwheels. The equestrians followed: the Fabulous Fentons wore bright blue and green costumes. Caped aerial artists in pink tights marched with arms raised as if to say, "We are here. Now the show can start." Lions in caged wagons were pulled by huge dappled draft horses.

And then, of course, came the elephants. Elephants draped with the rich fabrics of the Orient, tassels and bells swinging and glittering, advanced with an elegance at odds with their enormity. Women wearing wild feathered headdresses and risqué sequined tights rode on the elephants' shoulders while trunks were held high and undulated like giant serpents dancing to an Indian mystic's flute.

Zaza sat on top of Big Betty, a female elephant from Sri Lanka, possibly a cousin of Juliette's. Only one elephant carried no rider: the largest pachyderm in the procession—Romeo.

The full circus stood arrayed around the center ring. Clowns frolicked while the band played "The Stars and

Stripes" in a slightly discordant form. The elephants were nearest the bleachers. A group of rowdy teenagers sat in the front row across from Romeo, jeering and taunting the elephant. One of these ruffians, a tall, tomboyish girl was being especially abrasive.

"Where'd ya get that nose, ya old freak?" she heckled. "Yer just a big lump of dung, you are."

Now, elephants are among the smartest animals on earth—probably smarter than most humans. They have an extensive vocabulary and a good understanding of inflection in human speech patterns. Romeo was not pleased with this tall Amazon of a girl, not pleased at all. He turned and, it has to be qualified, gently—ever so gently slapped the young missy with his trunk. This set her back onto her derriere, which caused her companions to chortle and guffaw at the sight. She flung her hands wildly around, reaching back and finding the handle of a lady's umbrella which she promptly grabbed and, brandishing the bumpershoot like a Samurai sword, leaped across the flimsy barrier between the audience and the performing ring and took a swipe at the surprised elephant.

Tom Cavendish, who had been leading Romeo in the parade, shouted a warning to the girl but Romeo fended off the attack by winding his burly trunk around her. He lifted her high over his head as a unified gasp issued from the crowd. Then, as gentle as you please, he set her down upon the bleacher seat, abashed, embarrassed, and most likely happy to be alive.

But it was not over. There came a loud report, not unlike the firing of a pistol or a rifle. Tom gaped in alarm at the bizarre figure of a frown-faced clown with a red-slashed eye casting an ugly bullwhip behind him for a second lashing at Romeo.

"You devil!" yelled George Hershberger through his wrinkled grease paint.

"You bastard! Leave him alone!" shouted Tom.

"Bastard, am I? You, who would cuckold me with my Rose? You're the bastard!"

By this time Romeo had turned and was shuffling in place, like a long distant runner getting ready for the starting gun. Tom sensed the impending charge that would no doubt transform George Hershberger into a clown pancake and quickly stepped in front of Romeo. The elephant became calm once Tom's mewing reassurance reached his giant ears, but a fire of hatred burned in his eyes as he watched the clown sprinting away. The audience applauded, thinking it was all part of the act. It was only a prelude.

By November, the circus was back at winter quarters in Delavan, Wisconsin. Snow lacquered the town with a glossy sheen that bounced the brilliant winter sun into eyes lashed with frost. At night the waning moon cast faint shadows across ice-caked river beds. Out on the big lake loons circled in the morning mists and hoot owls took flight at the advent of night's dark shroud. The voices of circus animals complaining of the cold were muffled by the banging of wind-blown tree limbs striking weathered barn siding at Lake Lawn Farm.

That night the pulse of flickering kerosene lamps gurgled and sputtered in the barn, the lamps' fumes mingling with years of elephant smell, the scent of molding hay and dried bird droppings. Tom Cavendish had just finished pulling the iron latch shut on the door to Romeo's stall, a new, strong latch he hoped was elephant proof and would deter Romeo's nocturnal adventures. Snorting and stomping echoed through the barn as the elephants fussed nervously. Tom's own hackles rose as he sensed an unwelcome presence—something moving through the dim lantern light. Romeo pressed against the stall door, bending the thick wooden rails, but the latch held.

"Who's there?" asked Tom. Out of the shadows stepped George Herbert Hershberger, frozen breath pumping from his mouth in short bursts like a train engine building up steam.

"Now I've got you," said the interloper. "You've been with my wife for the last time."

Tom backed away from the large man. It was useless to try reason but perhaps, if he could wait him out.... He bumped against the barn's wall, rough wood and protruding nail heads scraping his back. He heard the man laugh a bitter and brutal laugh that made him shiver.

The clown magician, knife thrower and whip master reached under his jacket and brought out a throwing knife. This he hurled at Tom, pinning his left ear to the wall. Tom cried out in pain. The elephants trumpeted a poignant response. Another laugh from George Hershberger—almost a cackle, then another blade flew through the flickering lamp light and struck just to the right of Tom's throat: a few millimeters short of his jugular vein.

One, two, three more blades flew, outlining Tom's body against the barn wall. Each razor sharp knife lightly grazed his skin; the death of a thousand cuts? But his assailant paused and seemed to consider. Tom was immobile, pinned against the wall, unable to move for fear of tearing open an artery. It was too easy.

"The knife is too quick a death for you, wife stealer!" he said and reached for the coiled bull whip hanging at his waist. "I'll flail you into little pieces!"

As George Hershberger uncoiled the whip behind him, ready for the first blow, a third player crept into the barn, eager to enact a roll she had long practiced in her imagination. Zaza had trailed George to the barn, mayhem on her mind. She held a single action Colt 45 in one trembling hand. She raised the gun but faltered. The trigger seemed to be made of cast iron, impossible to pull. Her spirit sank. Suddenly, she knew what she had to do. She moved to the stall door and jerked back the latch, releasing Romeo.

The elephant didn't hesitate. His trunk coiled around the whip master, constricting, crushing air from lungs, splintering ribs. The man was lifted high above the elephant's head and tossed to land in a broken, twisted heap. He never regained consciousness.

George Hershberger became yet another accident statistic on the circus' books. It happened all the time: people got too close to the big cats or fell from the high wire. In the east, a so-called killer elephant would probably be destroyed, but here, in the circus colony of Delavan, Wisconsin, winter home to 26 circuses, there were no killer elephants, or killer tigers, or killer monkeys. Human life might be cheap, but animals cost good money.

Rose moved in with Tom. When the circus closed down,

they settled down in Delavan, Tom opening a hardware store on Walworth Street. Years later, Zaza left for Chicago, where the World's Columbian Exposition was about to open and organized a troupe of exotic dancers to perform at the fair's Streets of Paris exhibit. Romeo died in Ohio from a foot infection that couldn't be stemmed. His body was deposited unceremoniously at the city dump. Some said he was mad. Others knew the real truth.

ONE FALSE SPRING

That afternoon, late in what had been a mild Midwestern winter, the surrounding landscape seemed a blank but muddy canvas, ready for any dab of brightness to challenge the doldrums of the day. Piles of dirty snow remained under bushes and in the shade cast by imposing Victorian houses, aging but steadfast refugees from an more elegant era, houses which lined the main street of Delavan, Wisconsin. Squirrels scurried, relentlessly unearthing walnuts, fall buried, husks rotting in the dank thaw of a false spring. Canadian geese circled in the gray sky above, their persistent blaring creating a pompous ambiance somehow discordant, out of tune and out of place at this particular point in time.

Sally Owen lived alone in the pink and green corner house with its turret and sprawling porch. Not a dog, cat, bird or fish shared her domicile or her solitude. There were times when the emptiness of the huge house overwhelmed her. She would not sit on the wicker rocker on the porch to enjoy the mild afternoon because being in that vast open space seemed to increase her isolation.

Perhaps it was the rambling wooden flooring that stretched in every direction that created a kind of void in which she seemed to float. Or perhaps it was the delicate turned balusters like the spindly bars of a cage which made her feel exposed, a frail bird with clipped wings. She sought instead the small enclosed porch off the kitchen at the back of the house where she could sit stiffly on a hard wooden bench and sip acrid over-brewed tea from an old chipped cup.

If asked to speculate, Sally's neighbors would have said she was about 45, give or take a few years. She was much younger. Her appearance, in rumpled house coat or old jeans and sweatshirt betrayed the decade or so by which the estimates had missed her true age. The way she held her shoulders in a mournful slump added to the betrayal. She lived simply, on an inheritance from her parents. There were no siblings to share with so the whole of the house and a substantial, but not unlimited estate had gone to Sally. She had little incentive to search for employment where socializing with co-workers might have lifted her spirits. She considered herself content yet an emptiness dominated her life, eventually reaching the magnitude of an ache that would not subside.

The boy had crawled on hands and knees through the thickest part of the garden dodging clumps of snow and frozen dirt. Dastardly pirates pursued him. Their trained geese flew overhead, broadcasting his location with honks and hoots. He could feel them closing in. A tall pillar speckled with green moss loomed ahead.

Perched on top was the object of his quest: the great silver orb, its mirror-like surface reflecting the broken brambles and crushed brush surrounding him. Its magic would transport him instantly to a joyful new world where danger could not follow—if only he could reach out and touch it. He stood and his arm encircled the pillar but age and weather had rendered it a precarious platform and it tottered, toppling the great silver orb which shattered into myriad shards at his feet. He scooped up a handful of shards, wincing as the thin glass sliced into his palm. As dark red blood began to spread the boy began to wail and sob intermittently, harmonizing with the honking geese. A second shock came when he saw the woman standing over him, her face twisted into a foreboding scowl.

"Come with me, boy," she said.

He followed her up some stairs and into a house. She sat him down at the kitchen table while she went for bandages and Mercurochrome. He felt he might faint. The chair rocked on the uneven linoleum floor. She reappeared, took him to the sink where she held his wounded hand under the tap, the cold water stinging as blood swirled around and down the drain.

"Not so bad," she said as she swabbed the cut with Mercurochrome, pressed a fresh gauze pad against it then taped it securely.

"I'm sorry I bleeded on your table," said the boy. His sobbing had subsided and the room no longer threatened to spin around him.

"What's your name, boy? How old are you? Where do you live? What were you doing in my garden?" The questions came too fast and again he felt faint. She saw this and said, "Put you head down if you feel faint. It's all right."

Sally Owen had heard the crash as she sat on her back porch. Looking out across the garden she had seen a small boy. At first she thought she would chase him away. Then she saw that he was crying, staring at his hand which was red with blood. At that instant something stirred in Sally's breast. She teetered on the cusp of change. Where before she had been mired in inaction and ambivalence, she now felt a strange urge to rush to the aid of this boy. Some hidden instinct had awakened, certainly not maternal, but one she feebly fought against and was unable to overcome.

Now in the kitchen she studied the boy. Blond, towheaded, he might have stepped from the pages of *Snip, Snap and Snur*. He was gangly, perhaps tall for his age of 7 or 8. His jacket which now hung over a ladder back chair and the clothes he wore were spotted with mud—there seemed to be more dirt than boy.

She ran cold water onto a wash cloth, rang it out and pressed it to his forehead. He shivered. She tried to reassure him telling him not to worry about having broken the gazing globe. It was old and the wind would have blown it over eventually. Maybe he would like some hot chocolate? It would only take a moment.

As Sally heated milk in a pan on the stove the boy looked around the room. Faded flowered wall paper covered the walls. Here and there were hung copper molds that probably had not been used since the flowers on the wallpaper had bloomed bright. In his mind's eye he saw the stone walls of a castle, the metal things were the shining shields of long dead knights, displayed to honor their memory. He was the last of those knights, wounded in a battle with a fearsome dragon. Victorious, now he was being rewarded by her majesty, the queen. She presented him with a golden chalice.

"Would you like some marshmallows in your hot chocolate?" Sally asked.

Sir Steven, for that was the knight's name, nodded in approval as the queen poured a handful of rare pearls into the golden chalice.

Sally tried hard to overcome her discomfort in interacting with the child. She felt responsible for his injury but carrying on small talk with this urchin who didn't talk at all was beyond her expertise. Plus, it was in her nature to shy away from personal discourse, regardless of the age of the respondent. In college she had been a loner, a wallflower at social occasions, even then as faded as those on the paper now in her kitchen. This had almost been reversed by the approaches of a young man whom Sally had admitted (to herself) was someone she could let inside her armor, someone she could communicate with—on any and every level. But fate and a Greyhound bus had altered the course of that potential romance by smashing into her parents' car one icy November night. Thus had ended college, true love, and any hope that Sally might look at life as a jubilant venture—a journey to be shared.

She had withdrawn even further into her shell, an action begun many years before that accident. An option had been removed: she could no longer confront her feelings of worthlessness because the obstacle blocking that path had been permanently cemented in place. Now, as she watched the boy slurping his chocolate, brown drops rolling down his dirty chin, memory of a reoccurring dream she had had came to her. Like a slender-necked swan dipping its head into a stagnant pond she thought she saw something in the murky depths of memory.

In the dream she stood on one side of a busy highway

somewhere in the mountains. On the other side was a man in a white robe who beckoned. As she tried to cross she found her legs heavy and sluggish. The noise of rushing cars and trucks mingled with the sound of a harsh wind which blew against her. Each step was an agonizing struggle against gravity. She could see the man shaking his head as if to reproach her for the sluggishness of her progress. A huge truck bore down on her as she dragged her deadened limbs across the road.

At this point in the dream she would normally awaken, bathed in sweat and breathing in gasps. But now, as she was already awake, she could exercise that unique aspect of consciousness: the ability to continue and finish the dream according to own her wakeful wishes, in defiance of her subconscious. And so it was that she crossed the road in safety and recognized the beckoning man.

Sir Steven saw the change in the queen's countenance. The eyes squinted and glistened with a wetness that might be heralding tears. Yet the slack mouth gradually broadened into a smile as the queen reached to grasp his hand. "Kevin," she cried, "You've come back!"

"No, Ma'am, I'm Stevie!"

"No, you're Kevin. I'd know you anywhere. You've come back! I don't know how, but you've come back to me. Oh, I missed you so much!"

"But, Ma'am...."

"Don't you know me? I'm your sister, Sally. Yes, I look older now. You...you haven't changed. Don't you remember? We weren't just brother and sister, we were best friends. We did everything together." She paused, squeezed the boy's hand tightly. The tears began to well, blurring her vision. She couldn't see the fear on the boy's face.

"They wouldn't let me come. I saw, you know. I saw you in the street. The car...they took you to the hospital. I know that. They wouldn't let me...they didn't answer my questions. When you didn't come back. They wouldn't let me ask...oh, but you've come back to me now! We can be together now. Kevin, Kevin..."

"Please, Ma'am. Please...I'm Stevie. I'm not Kevin," pleaded the boy. She came around the table to him. Her arms surrounded him, pressing him against her.

"It was him across the highway. It was Father. He wished it was me. Not you. They wouldn't let me ask."

Sir Steven watched in horror as the queen changed into the witch. She clutched at him, began to pull him toward the open stove where glowing coals waited to roast him, to turn him into a charred carcass. He thrashed about in her arms, finally breaking free, then bolted from the witch's castle. He ran, his armor clanking and weighing him down. The shards of the broken silver orb crunched under his boots. Above, in the gray sky, the witch's trained geese followed him. Flakes of wet snow began to fall. Winter had returned.

ERIK TAKES A TRIP

The man in the cell was naked. The metal bench on which he sat was cold against his skin. Iron bars one inch thick ran both vertically and horizontally across the only window in the small cell. Through this, the setting sun cast a checkerboard of orange swatches across the concrete floor: his only illumination in this dank, dark prison.

He stared at the heavy iron door; it seemed an impossible obstacle in the plan for escape that occupied his mind. The lock and the hinges of the door were accessible only from the outside. The only openings in the door were a rectangular slot used to slide a tray of food to the prisoner and a peephole the size of a fist.

His eyes fell upon his wrists where a glint of light reflected from metal shackles. These were specially designed to fit tightly, preventing the prisoner from slipping his hands through the cuffs. The lock, requiring a custom-made key, could not be picked. Yet, despite these impossible odds, the man felt relaxed, confident. He slowed his breathing, letting his lungs expand fully.

The metal bands restraining him prompted a memory. As a child he had witnessed police leading men through the streets who were shackled with similar devices. This bizarre parade had followed the tragic deaths of seven people when guardsmen had fired into a crowd of striking workers.

He remembered those days in the spring of 1886, the

thousands of Polish and German laborers moving from factory to factory, shutting down the plants one by one, swelling their numbers until 14,000 of them brought industry in Milwaukee to a standstill. Their goal, an eight-hour workday.

He remembered too, seeing the fallen. One of those killed in what would come to be called the Bay View Massacre was a boy about his own age. He thought he recognized the boy but the blood and gore made identification difficult. He was twelve years old that year.

Erik Weisz had been born in Budapest, Hungary, in 1874. His family had immigrated to the United States when he was four. His father brought them to Appleton, Wisconsin, where he became one of that growing town's first rabbis. The family name was changed to Weiss, and Erik became Ehrich.

By 1883 the Weiss family found itself in Milwaukee, struggling to survive in those hard economic times. Mayer Samuel Weiss, Ehrich's father, worked as a schochet—a rabbi who ceremoniously butchers animals to produce kosher meats. Ehrich contributed by shining shoes and selling newspapers. Not unlike the many German and Jewish immigrants that poured into Milwaukee in the nineteenth century, they were poor.

The year of the Bay View Massacre, Ehrich decided to travel. He would journey out into the world, find work, and come of age independently. He was confident, eager, and perhaps a little naïve, but ready for adventure and excitement. Grabbing his shoeshine kit he walked to the freight yards and waited until a train began slowly pulling away. He ran along side of a boxcar with an open door, tossed his kit in and leaped after it. Soon the train picked up speed, rumbled out of Milwaukee and was heading west through the rural Wisconsin countryside.

Eddies of dust and bits of straw swirled up inside the boxcar stinging Ehrich's eyes and setting him to coughing. He crouched back against the wall and watched as trees and fields swung past the open door. Black and white spotted cows were bunched together in muddied pastures, looking like a bedraggled army on a parade ground.

Ehrich Weiss was called "Ehrie" for short. As he began

his odyssey he made another decision: he would become Harry—Harry White. No longer a Jewish immigrant from Budepest, he would now be Harry White from Appleton. He wondered how long it would take the train to get to California or Texas or...

Ninety minutes after leaving Milwaukee, the train pulled into Delavan. Curious to see this small Wisconsin town which was the winter quarters of many of the Midwest's most famous circuses, Harry jumped out of the boxcar and walked toward the downtown.

He turned down Walworth Avenue, past the barber shop and the billiard hall and approached some men standing outside of Hill's Grocery. Did they want a shoe shine, he asked? Not today, they answered. He continued down Walworth past the offices of the Delavan Republican, past the meat market, Dorn's Taylor Shop, the Citizens' Bank and Berg's Drug store, offering his services to those he found loitering on the wooden sidewalk, but was unable to find anyone to hire him.

On the next block were a feed store, a stove merchant's and a dental college while across the street loomed the large Hollinger and Calkins Livery, the Delavan Hotel and a harness shop. Quite a thriving community, thought Harry White. Unfortunately, nobody here seemed to have dirty shoes! He paused in front of Kelsey's Temple of Art, a photography studio, and gazed at the framed portraits in the window. A stern looking man with huge chin whiskers stared back at him from a gilded wooden frame.

Then down the street he spotted a group of soldiers standing in front of the Park Hotel whose signage announced that every room was equipped with gas lights. Certainly these men would need a shoe shine. These were some of the Delavan Guards, a company assigned to the First Regiment of the Wisconsin National Guard, under Col. William B. Britton. They had recently returned from Milwaukee where they had been called into service by Governor Rank "to preserve the peace and dignity of the state which was threatened by rioters in that city." Their orders had been to shoot to kill.

Harry approached the dozen or so guardsmen. He had to admire their uniforms: jackets neatly pressed with brass buttons, yellow braid on collar, chest and cuffs and Calvary-style trousers, dark blue with a yellow stripe. Yet there was something sinister about them. Perhaps it was their youth, their cynical demeanor, or the detachment with which they bantered. It was as if the outside world never penetrated their conviction that duty and polished brass ranked above congeniality. Or perhaps they were soured by recent events.

He opened his shoeshine kit and extracted a soiled rag and a tin of polish. Brandishing these, he said to the guards, "Who will be the first to get the best shoeshine this side of Lake Michigan?" A few heads turned, cursory glances were given, but no one acknowledged him, no one took him up on his offer. Harry took the cloth in both hands and began snapping it in the air in a quick rhythm as he had seen colored boys do back on the streets of Milwaukee. "Aw, come on, men! Look your best with a great new shine!"

Hector Bennington had volunteered for the Delavan Guards soon after graduation from high school. He had been desperate to escape from the boredom of small town life. When his unit had been assigned to protect Milwaukee's railroad property during the labor disputes, Hector was elated. When they confronted the striking workers who had gathered in front of the Stanislas Church he was eager to engage them but disappointed when the company commander instructed them only to fire into the air above the crowd.

There had been eight-hour day demonstrations in other cities. In Chicago, at the Haymarket Square on that same day, someone had thrown a bomb killing seven policemen and wounding sixty people. Word of the incident spread to Milwaukee, raising tensions on both sides of the conflict. Hector's hatred of the Polish workers grew. When the strikers marched on the North Chicago Rolling Mill the next day, Hector positioned himself on the front line of the guards. This time, the order came to fire into the crowd.

Now Hector was being annoyed by a street urchin waving a shoeshine cloth and disrupting what little camaraderie there was to the idle chit-chat of the guardsmen. It was bad enough that the Temperance

Movement was so strong in Delavan; that the town's only tavern was crammed with itinerant circus people, limiting the recreational opportunities the guardsmen had for themselves. Now they had to be assailed by some child hawking services that were unnecessary to a good soldier who polished his own boots daily.

"Hey, you!" Hector yelled at Harry. "Beat it! Go somewhere else with your caterwauling!"

"Why, Sergeant," replied Harry, knowing full well that the guardsman had no rank, "you can't be leadin' the troops with boots that look like you've been marching through a bunch of cow pies."

Hector charged at Harry, picked up the shoeshine kit and heaved it into the street, scattering its contents. Harry retreated, gathering up tins of polish, brushes, and rags and stuffed them hastily into the box. As Hector continued to advance towards him, Harry ran.

Bud Flitcroft had turned fifteen last month. He had been looking for a summer job since school let out in June, but so far he was having about as much luck as Harry White was having shining shoes. It was late in the afternoon, approaching supper time, but he thought he should try one more place: the livery stable by the hotel. It was a smaller livery than the Hollinger and Calkins Livery, being primarily for the convenience of visitors to the Park Hotel, but he would leave no stone unturned.

The guardsmen Harry had encountered in front of the hotel were long gone and the street was deserted as Bud swung open the stable door. There didn't seem to be anyone present, save for a few horses snorting impatiently in their stalls and a large yellow cat with a notch out of its ear who yowled at him to protest his entry into its domain. He was about to leave when he noticed a pile of burlap bags in one corner and a small figure curled on top, apparently asleep.

He moved closer to examine the sleeping figure when suddenly, the sleeper awoke, sat up and said, "Oh, sorry. I was tired...I didn't mean to trespass."

"Don't worry," said Bud, "I'm not with the livery. Go back to sleep. I'm leaving."

"Wait," said the boy on the burlap. "Do you have

anything to eat?"

"Who are you, anyway? If you're hungry..."

"My name is Harry White. I've been on the road for...for some time now. I could tell you many stories about my travels. But I'm very hungry and I've no prospects for the present."

"Well, Harry White, you better come along home with me. My mother will certainly invite you to dinner once she hears your story. By the way, my name is Bud...Bud Flitcroft. I live not too far from here."

The Flitcrofts lived in a modest two story farm house on south Sixth Street, just beyond the railroad tracks. There were days when the house shook noticeably from the passage of freight trains and the yard filled up with soot from the engines. Bud loved it when the circuses loaded their animals on freight cars at the depot two blocks away. Elephants, camels, caged lions and tigers and bears—it was the stuff of a young boy's fantasy: to run away and join the circus!

Thomas and Hannah had married in 1856 and moved into the charming house on the other side of the tracks (in Delavan, Wisconsin, neither side of the tracks was the "wrong side") where they raised three children. Ellen was the eldest, followed by Tom Junior, and then Bud, whose given name was Alfred. It was a close-knit family, and Bud's mother, Hannah, was especially big hearted.

Hannah took to the boy, Harry White, immediately. He was fed and Hannah saw that he found his way to the brass bath tub on the back porch for a good scrubbing. Harry could stay with the Flitcrofts, she said, until he found work or decided to return home. "Home? I haven't a home," said Harry. "You have now," answered Mrs. Flitcroft.

Harry made the rounds with Bud, enquiring at various places of business downtown, but as Bud had already learned, there was no work for young boys these days, not at the millinery, not at the drug store, not at the stables.

"Why don't we try the circuses?" asked Harry. "Surely they need someone to feed and water the elephants."

"They are mostly on the road now. It's summer. They come back to Delavan for the winter. Then they train the animals in big barns down by the lake. Sometimes one of the elephants gets loose and runs through town! People hide because there are stories of elephants killing people."

"I saw a circus once," said Harry. "Back in Milwaukee. There was this magician who cut off a woman's arms and legs and then reattached them! It was glorious!"

"That's just a trick. An illusion."

"Of course. But it's fun to watch and pretend it's real."

Bud's sister, Ellen, had a girl friend named Betsy Tollinger. Betsy lived on the other side of the tracks in a large Queen Anne Victorian house with a long, wrap-around front porch. The girls, in their late teens, liked to sit on the porch on a glider, and watch people walking or in carriages, on their way to or from the downtown. Often, they attracted the attention of young men passing by.

Betsy was attracted to one of the Delavan Guards in his elegant uniform: a young man named Hector Bennington. It was the same Hector Bennington who had accosted Harry White in front of the Park Hotel. Hector had asked Betsy to step out with him. There were dances down at the Lake Lawn Hotel but Betsy's father wouldn't allow her to go. It was a sore point with Hector.

On this particular day, Ellen and Betsy were sitting on the front porch as Harry and Bud walked by. Ellen waved to them and they climbed the wooden steps past tendrils of wisteria that coiled around the balustrades. Ellen introduced Harry to Betsy. Harry bowed. Betsy smiled. Harry demonstrated a tap-dancing step rather badly. Betsy laughed. Bud pulled on Harry's arm. "Let's go," he said.

In the weeks that followed Harry and Betsy became—not a couple, as she was 18 and he only 12, but companions with a mutual enchantment—he for her and she for him. Betsy found the young boy energetic and amusing, clever and creative, with no end of ideas for innocent mischief. Harry was intrigued by the older girl. She was not exactly a mother figure for him, more of a big sister or second cousin who was unabashed at revealing her feelings and anxieties about life. Together they explored possibilities for adventure in the quiet burg of Delavan.

Betsy was comfortable in the presence of the younger boy, much more at ease than she had been with the likes of Hector Bennington. Bennington had excited her in a way she disliked: a loss of control she was unused to, the pull of desire which could only lead in an unknown and unwanted direction. The boy, Harry, was like a real live doll with whom she could play act, rehearsing fantastic scenarios without fear of ridicule or embarrassment. There was a naïve eroticism to their relationship that neither fully understood.

One day Betsy suggested that Harry take her swimming at the Mill Pond, a favorite swimming hole near the east branch of the Turtle Creek where locals sometimes congregated in the hot days of the Wisconsin summer. Harry replied that he didn't have a swimming suit. He had arrived in Delavan with only the clothes on his back and although Mrs. Flitcroft had bought some apparel for him, a swimming suit wasn't part of his current wardrobe.

"What do you need a suit for, anyway?" asked Betsy.

The Mill Pond was a spring-fed pool about fifty yards long and half as wide, rimmed with bull-rushes in which frogs sang in discordant harmonies. Tall willows lined the nearby creek, their long swaying branches reflecting in the gently rippling pond. Harry stripped to his briefs and flexed his arms in a parody of a strong man. Betsy laughed.

As Betsy began to undress a familiar and unwelcome figure appeared. Hector Bennington, in his civilian clothes, stood scowling and clinching his fists.

"Isn't this just lovely," Hector blurted. "Being a bit risk-kay ain't you?"

"Hector, leave us alone. We're just here to swim," said Betsy.

"Ya. Go polish yer boots," snipped Harry.

Hector's pride was hurt. Rejected by the object of his affections in front of this...this boy! This would not do. With a sudden rush of anger Hector grabbed the boy in a bear-hug and jerked him off his feet. "So go swimming, then," he cried and began to swing Harry out toward the water.

"No! No, I can't swim," lied Harry. But it was too late. Hector flung the boy into the pond with a huge splash. Harry went under, and then surfaced, flailing his arms and calling for help. Hector just grinned widely, satisfied that his revenge was now complete.

Harry slipped beneath the surface, releasing a little stream of bubbles. Betsy screamed. Then she yelled at Hector: "Jump in and save him, you...you..."

"OK. Ok. I'm going to." Hector pulled off his shoes and leaped into the pond. The water was too muddy to see anything but he dived under the surface and felt around where Harry had last been seen. He spent several minutes searching but returned to the shore unsuccessful and very wet.

"He's gone. He must have drowned," said Hector. "No one could hold their breath this long."

"We have to go for help. Get the police or somebody," Betsy said, sobbing.

"You go. I'm leaving." With that insensitive response, Hector Bennington turned and ran. Betsy watched him go in disbelief. What a coward he was! What a villain! She looked back at the pond, tears beginning to cascade down her cheeks. Suddenly the surface of the pond stirred, broke as a round form emerged.

"Harry!"

"Hi, Betsy," said Harry White, gulping down mouthfuls of air. "Is he gone yet?"

"Harry...you...you said you couldn't swim! I thought you were drowned!"

"Ah, don't be worried, I can swim alright. And hold my breath too! I used to practice seeing how long I could hold it. Came in real handy, I'd say."

That was not the last they would see of Hector. As autumn approached, Harry and Betsy explored the paths along the creek as well as the back alleys in the town. Harry had spotted a deserted building on Main Street, which was being used for storage by one of the circuses. Through dust shrouded windows he could just barely make out the exotic shapes of circus paraphernalia, stacks of clothing, coils of rope, intricate headdresses once worn by elephants.

"Let's go in," he said to Betsy. His eager grin only confused the girl.

"It's all locked up," she answered.

"My mother," Harry started to explain, never failing to make a short story long, "used to bake the best apple pies in the world! She knew me and my brothers would eat the pies before they even cooled off so she tried to lock them up in a closet just off the kitchen. Well, I liked those pies so much that I just had to get that door open. I found a bent piece of wire and started probing around inside the lock. After a few false starts I figured out how the lock worked and I was able to pick it! Never went hungry for pies after that."

They found a back door in the alley behind the building. Harry went to work on the lock and soon there was a loud click as the latch yielded to his expertise. They looked in all directions, and it appeared that the coast was clear: no one was around to see them breaking and entering. No one, that is, except Hector Bennington who had been following them that day.

Inside was a magical world of sequined fabrics and garishly painted objects whose purpose was not readily discernable. Large wooden boxes on which lions and tigers might have perched, yards and yards of canvas with illustrations of strange monsters—an alligator boy, a missing link—and twisted metal rods that must have once been the bars of a cage. There was a box of old posters and another of old ticket stubs. A battered tuba leaned against one wall, a testimony to a bygone day before the calliope appeared on the scene.

"Look over there," said Harry. He pointed to a heavy iron door that stood open. "It's a walk-in safe!" The building, they speculated, must have once been a bank, for here was a small room with thick cement walls and with a door that would close and lock securely, protected by a rotary dial that would open only by a special combination of numbers.

"Let's go inside!" Harry pulled Betsy along with him and entered the musty-smelling chamber. Cobwebs hung from the walls and ceiling. A carpet of dust lay on the floor. Harry produced a box of matches from his pocket and struck a Lucifer against the wall. White phosphorus flared and illuminated the safe. It was empty.

Just as they turned to exit the safe the door closed with a heavy thud. They pushed against it but it would not budge. There was a rattling noise and Harry realized, to his horror, that someone was twisting the dial on the combination lock. They were trapped inside an old safe in a deserted building. And no one knew they were there. No one, except Hector Bennington, and he wasn't about to tell anyone.

Harry struck another match. "Yep, it's a combination lock," he said.

"Can't you pick it?" asked Betsy.

"Not this kind of a lock, Betsy. Ouch!" The match had burned done to his finger tips. Swiftly, Harry lit another and began to study the inside of the lock. "You know," he said, "these things were designed to keep people from breaking *into* the vault. All we have to do is to break *out*."

"I don't understand."

"Look. It works by a series of wheels—see there are three of them. They have to rotate so they line up these notches along the top where this bar can drop into the notches. That releases a catch and the lock will open. Ouch!"

"Here, let me hold the next match."

"I think I can do it by feel...in the dark. We don't want to burn up all our air. This might take a little time to figure out."

It only took Harry White ten minutes to manipulate the wheels of the combination lock. The trick was to start by lining up the wheel closest to him, then turning the next in the opposite direction until he heard a click. Keeping the two wheels aligned, he then rotated all three back in the other direction, waiting for the click.

"That was pretty easy," he said. "I could probably do it from the outside just as well. Hey! I would make a good bank robber!"

"Oh, Harry, don't joke about such things!"

The story of how Harry White came to be sitting naked in a jail cell is a long and very interesting one, but perhaps better told by someone else. Harry eventually left Delavan, Wisconsin, and traveled to Saint Louis, Missouri, where he found work in a necktie factory, cutting out patterns. After two years of traveling, the runaway returned home. Still fascinated by the stage magic he had seen at the circus, he began performing for children in the neighborhood. He could swing by his knees from a trapeze and pick up straight pins with his eye lids. He called himself the Prince of the Air. As his career as an illusionist evolved he tried out a variety of names: He was Eric The Great, Cardo, Professor Murat, King of Cards, World's Handcuff King and Prison Breaker, The Greatest Necromancer of the Age, and The Master Mystifier.

Although he did card tricks, disappearing acts and even mastered the illusion of cutting a woman's arms and legs off, then reattaching them, he found that his greatest talent was as an escape artist. As he embarked upon this new career, he began calling himself Harry Houdini.

MY COUSIN JEANIE

There are some summer vacations you have as a kid that stick in your memory. I remember, for instance, a trip to the Wisconsin Dells in the early 1950s when we watched a dog make an impossible jump from a cliff to a stone pillar called the Standing Rock. There used to be a man that made that jump, but I guess it became too dangerous, so they substituted a German Shepard.

We took vacations to Wisconsin many times, often to visit my aunt and uncle and my cousins in Superior, Wisconsin, the very top of the world. The year we went to the Dells, though, was special. The natural beauty of the place was not lost on us children. It was if we had traveled to some alien place—like Mars!

But as spectacular as the Dells was, there was another place that will stick forever in my memory. It was just as alien and exotic and it was closer to home: Riverview Park on Chicago's West Side. It was so fascinating and alluring that my cousins from Superior coerced their parents into visiting us several summers in a row just so they could go there. One summer when my cousin Jeanie...but I'm getting ahead of my story. Let me tell it from the perspective of my thirteen-year-old self of those years.

My name is Lonnie Olson. I live in a suburb of Chicago. I have a brother named Jack who is two years older than I am. When Pop moved us from Andersonville, Chicago's Swedish district, to suburban Downers Grove in 1948, the only thing concerning my brother Jack and I was whether or not the natives played stickball. Perhaps it took a while to acclimate to our new environment, perhaps the slow pace of the place gave us a chance to catch our breaths, look at the world in a new way. Eventually we became as suburban as...well...as mowed lawns, paved sidewalks and one-car garages.

The promise of green lawns and fresh air had lured Mom and Pop away from big city dust, rats and pigeons. Eager instead to embrace squirrels and gophers, Pop had quit his job at the bakery and poured his life savings into a down payment on a little post-war cape cod. My father was ambitious. He would make a new life for himself and his family away from the sprawl and smell of the city.

Pop became a grease monkey. The smell of dried motor oil preceded him into the living room when he came home from work. The gas station had been built in the late 1920's, when automobiles were just beginning to change the cultural logistics of America. It didn't have lifts, instead it had pits where Pop would stand under the cars to lube and change their oil. His six-foot-two stature caused him to stoop a little, a circumstance that would eventually result in chronic back pain, but he never complained.

My brother Jack discovered Pony League baseball. I didn't share his new passion so I loitered at the station after school. Cars all looked alike then, not yet having exploded into the bizarre, science fiction designs the '50s would bring. I memorized the insignias on those great metal boats so that I could recognize them on the street. Buicks were the most fascinating with their great grinning grills and phony side holes. Bumpers were chrome structures you could fantasize were parts of Flash Gordon space ships or shining futuristic cityscapes. I liked cars. I liked to hang out at the gas station. I liked Ollie.

Ollie is a rough old Swede who works with Pop. This day, rimless cap and oily soaked shirt, he is emerging from the pit like some prehistoric creature struggling out of the tar.

"Hi, kid. Have you seen the new one?" he taunts me. The new one is a wrecked car, ceremoniously dragged from the highway to be placed on display at the vacant corner by the station. This was the local custom whenever there was a really bad automobile accident.

"Ja, it's a doozie. A coupla darkies out from the city tried to drive it under a semi. Made a convertible out of her!"

Rushing to the wreck I can see that they haven't cleaned it up yet. There is always the hope of seeing body parts, and this time I'm not disappointed. Globs of blackish blood adorn the seats and something gray and spongy lies on the arm rest. And, it is a Buick! I'll be the first to report the gory scene at school in the morning, Of course, it isn't as spectacular as when Rick Jamison saw a severed hand still gripping the steering wheel of the old blue dodge that had flipped and rolled down Parkington's hill. But then, you couldn't always believe Rick Jamison.

Dinner at the Olson's (that's us) is one of the only times we are all together. This night my mother has cooked something she calls "Spanish Weenies," hot dogs split from end to end and boiled in a large cast iron skillet filled with stewed tomatoes from a can. Pop will never let her cook Swedish, so the weenies are her pathetic attempt at cooking ethnic, though I'll never understand what is "Spanish" about the dish.

"Eva, I have a plan," says Pop turning to my mother who is wiping her tomato stained hands on her flowered apron.

"Ja, I'm going to start a business."

"Pop!" blurted Jack, "Our team won today. I hit a double and..."

"Don't be interruptin' your father!" Mom would later say she'd had it up to here with Jack's impetuousness and inconsideration, although she wouldn't say that to Pop.

"Oh let the boy speak. After all he'll be joining me in the business. Take it over someday when I'm gone." Jack joining Pop? Not me? This is the first serious hint I have had of my actual position in the family. Jack, after all, was the oldest, but...

"Aw, Pop! I want to play baseball!"

"You'll do as your father says, Jackie. What's this business, Johann?"

"Fuel oil. I'm going to buy it in the summer when it's cheap, store it and get rich selling it in the winter!"

"But, Johann, people use coal!"

"No, Eva—oil is the future. You'll see."

"Pop," I call out from behind my plate of Spanish Weenies, "did you see the new wreck today? Blood and brains all over..."

"Hush, Lonnie" says Mom, scowling. "That's no good dinner table talk." Turning to Pop she says, "Ellen and Roy are bringing the kids down from Superior next week after school is out. It's spring vacation and the kids'll want to go to Riverview."

"Awk!" cries Pop. "Now I'll have to drive them screaming brats into Chicago on Ogden Avenue. Two hours drive," he complains.

Jack and I flash secret grins at each other. Once a year my Aunt and Uncle would drive down with our cousins, Jimmy and Jeanie, and my father would be forced to drive us all to Riverview Amusement Park at Western and Belmont in Chicago.

The park called itself the "World's Largest Amusement Park" where you could "laugh your troubles away." Pop hated the drive. It would be hot in the car and the series of Black neighborhoods we'd pass through made him nervous. We didn't care. We could smell the cotton candy and hear the clatter of wheels against steel rails from the Bobs, the world's fastest roller coaster. We could almost see the great canvas drapes painted red and yellow with pictures of the Alligator girl, the Snake Charmer and, of course, the Tattooed Lady, that lined the midway and served both as advertisements and as tent coverings for the various shows we wouldn't be allowed to see.

The next day after school I take the gang, who are Rick Jamison, Pete Meyers, Jerry Swanson and myself, to see the wreck but it's been hosed down and it's as clean as a hound's tooth.

"Oh ya, so where's the brains? You borrow 'em for yourself?"

"Seeing spots again, Lonnie?"

"Ha! Lonnie's just got a hard on for blood and guts an' he's seeing things!" This last from Rick, my sometimes best friend.

"Liar, liar, pants on fire," they all chant as they leave me moping and mortified. There's nothing to do but saunter over to the station to see Ollie.

Ollie has a 55 gallon drum of oil down off the old pickup. These weigh over 700 pounds so you wrestle them very carefully. He tips it on edge and walks it into the station's bay exhibiting little more effort than had he been pushing a baby carriage. He lets it fall horizontally onto a metal frame. The heavy thud sends dust into the air. He unscrews the small cap on the top of the drum and a silky stream of oil pours out into a smaller can, luminous against the darkness of the bay. I've told him about the taunting I've had from my companions.

"Them kids is a caution, don't you worry about them."

Ollie grabs me around the neck and I get a Dutch rub which is administered with the knuckles of his first and second fingers against my skull as if he is eradicating some unseen spot of dirt on a piece of cloth. My head will smart for the rest of the day.

Downers Grove is primarily a German town with a few Swedes and Norwegians and more migrating out from Chicago practically every day. There aren't any Blacks, Hispanics, Native Americans, Italians, Irish, Russians, Jews, Polish, Chinese (except for Chan of Chan's Chinese Laundry and his family), Japanese, Koreans, or East Indians, and very few Catholics. Mom and Pop are very comfortable with this. They don't mention it, but we know.

And Pop is comfortable at Riverview Park because he knows that Blacks are excluded there as they have been since its opening in 1913. No Blacks that is, except for Popeye.

Popeye is a tall burly Black man with a kindly face like your Uncle Henry. He dresses in baggy clothes and you can almost hear the blues when you look at him. He works on the midway at Riverview and for a quarter you can watch him pop his eyeballs out of their sockets—not all the way out and hanging down his checks, but enough that it looks like two big golf balls with dark spots have been glued to his face. Up to this time, Popeye is my sole experience of Black Chicago.

The front gate at Riverview is enough to kick start your imagination into a long-ago world of the Orient. It is a good three stories high with two enormous towers topped with those Arabian acorn roofs and supporting a forty foot arch. It is covered in red, white and blue bunting. Pop has brought the four of us, cousins Jimmy and Jeanie, my brother Jack and me, to Riverview, leaving Mom to entertain my aunt and uncle. Once through the gate, my cousin Jimmy and my brother Jack take off down the midway leaving Jeanie and me with Pop.

I'll get stuck riding the Ferris Wheel and the wimpy Silver Streak roller coaster with Jeanie while Jimmy and Jack will get to ride the Bobs (you must be this tall to ride, the sign with its ominous ruler reported). I can just see them, waiting in line by the large poster board filled with women's single earrings found in the cars, which serves to advertise and to warn of the wild ride to come. They will run for the front car, sit up very straight so that when the operator pulls back the safety bar there will be room to wiggle. When the car finishes its slow climb to the first hill they will stand up in their seats as the car plunges down the first great incline. The Bobs is supposed to reach speeds of 100 miles per hour and at one point makes a dive into a dark tunnel. At least one boy has fallen from it to his death in years past and there are always rumors of tragic accidents. This only heightens Jimmy's and Jack's shared teenage death wish.

"Pop, can we go to Aladdin's Castle?" I ask.

"That's too scary for Jeanie."

"No, it's not. I've been through it before!"

"Well. Okay, just this one time."

At the other end of the midway is the fun house called Aladdin's Castle. Its façade is a giant head and shoulders likeness of Aladdin, straight from the Arabian Nights. His wide eyes gaze seductively up the midway and roll back and forth. His eyebrows are raised as if to say, "Come into my parlor."

Pop deposits us at the ticket booth, gives us money and ambles off to find Jimmy and Jack. I don't tell him where they are. Inside are darkened narrow hallways that twist and turn. Sometimes the floor rocks back and forth; sometimes waxwork spiders light up and jump at you. There is a hall of mirrors. There is a gallery where you walk across a blast of air that blows up woman's skits and men can sit and watch. I am glad that Jeanie has worn slacks.

The air smells of mold and old sweat. You don't want to touch the walls. When a laughing skull lights up, Jeanie screams and falls back onto me. My hand touches the soft mound of her breast and my world suddenly changes. Jeanie is no longer the little imp that played in my sandbox and tormented me by following me around. There is a long hesitation as we stand there in the dark, unmoving and unspeaking. The skull lights up again. We both laugh and scramble up the hallway to the exit where the barrel roll awaits us. Tumbling out of the barrel and into the musty afternoon I see them: Rick, Pete and Jerry.

"Ha-ha. Lonnie's got a girl friend."

"I do not!"

"Who's that, your mother?"

"This is Jeanie, my cousin.

"Oh, kissing cousins?"

I have turned bright red and Jeanie is pulling at my arm. "Let's go," she says.

"Hey Lonnie, want to do the Parachute Jump?"

"I don't think my father..."

"Aw, come on, I dare ya. I double dare ya."

I look at Jeanie and she is giving me that "Can we please?" look. Besides, I've been dared and I can't back down. We follow the gang along the midway toward the jump. I only hope Pop doesn't see me.

Unknown to me at this time Pop is trying to pacify the park guard who has quarantined Jimmy and Jack after having seen them standing upright on the Bobs. I still have money left over and I buy a ticket.

"I'm going too," Jeanie says and I can tell by her serious face that I had better comply so I buy another ticket. I look over at the gang, but they are edging back from the ticket booth.

"What's the matter," I ask.

"Uh, Pete's father is over there. We can't go, but you guys can."

"What do you say, Jeanie?"

"These guys are chicken shit," she says. I'm shocked to hear my cousin swear, but I see we have the advantage.

We'll go up on the Parachute Jump and they'll forever be chicken shits. However, they are leaving now and I realize they won't be here to witness our act of bravado.

The Parachute Jump is a steel-girded tower rising several hundred feet high, like a cross between the Eiffel Tower and a giant octopus. It was supposed to have been used for training paratroopers during the war and then the park bought it. Real parachutes are attached to wires hanging from beams at the top of the tower. The parachutes are hauled up along the wires until they reach the top and are then released to free fall down, running along flimsy guide wires. Since they run along the wires there isn't any danger of them blowing away and the riders' weight pulls them down. As we wait we watch parachutes reaching the top and releasing, free falling a few feet until the parachute opens and then drifting lightly down to earth. There is a short instance before the chute opens that your stomach will be in your mouth.

When our turn comes I am expecting to be strapped in but the seat is just a wooden plank resembling a child's swing, big enough for two people. There are no seat belts. There's a little belt that goes over your lap but you could easily slip under it and plummet 200 feet to the pavement below, your head bursting open and your brains and blood spraying the crowd. Or you could be skewered on one of those Arabian acorn roofs.

The two ropes supporting the seat have been wrapped in black slippery tape so many times that I can't get my 13 year old hands around them. Jeanie hangs on to me and I squeeze the ropes as hard as I can. There has clearly been a mistake. This just can't be right. At least I won't die a total virgin. At least I have touched Jeanie's breast.

The parachute rises slowly. The ground falls away from us and the crowd begins to shrink. We can see the whole park now: the Shoot-the-Chutes water ride, the Rotor, the Tilt-A-Whirl, even the Bobs. The midway with its red and yellow banners stretches endlessly before us. There is a marching band coming along the midway and its brassy sounds are faint on the wind that whips up at us. We can see the buildings of the city and a splash of gold against the deep blue of Lake Michigan. Above us, the top of the tower is approaching where the chute will catch, hang and then drop. My fear has almost been overtaken by my awe. Almost. Jeanie is clinging hard to me and my hands are sweating.

There is the bump of metal against metal and we are suspended above the midway, above the city, above the smallness of adolescence. I don't think I'll be playing double dare anymore. Some kind of clear-headedness finds me and I momentarily feel brave and responsible for Jeanie. I almost say, "It's all right." Almost.

There is a click and we are dropping. The free fall lasts a few seconds but they feel more like hours. There is a jerk which almost tears my hands from the ropes. The chute has opened and our decent slows to a pleasant pace. Now is the time to relax, to look at the view, to smile at Jeanie and feel alive once again. Only something causes the parachute to fold over upon itself. We begin to drop again!

There is probably a time in everyone's life when they are forced to see the ugliness of impending disaster. It might thrill some, it might anger others, it must certainly frighten most. I felt all of those things and more. I had grown today and now I was to be broken. I would lose all that my new knowledge promised. I would be dead and no hero. I wouldn't know if Pop was successful in his new business. I wouldn't see Jack join the army and fight in Korea. I would never have another Dutch rub. There is a sound from Jeanie which might be a gasp or a sob. I feel my hands slipping.

And then, the chute opens again. We float to the ground. I am shaking. I jump from the ride and run down the gangway. I collide with a tall Black man with a kindly face. It is Popeye. He hugs me and tells me something I don't hear. Time can no longer be calculated by my brain so I don't know how long I stand there clinging to him, trembling. I look up to his face and he pops his eyeballs out. I begin to laugh. I am all right again. Jeanie is next to me, laughing and pulling at my arm.

"It's all right," she says.

My cousins had returned to their home in Superior, Wisconsin. School started. I was able to gain some points with the gang, having braved the Parachute Jump, without having to admit I had panicked. To this day I harbor an aversion toward amusement park rides. When I take my own children to the County Fair now-a-days I refuse to go on the wild rides with them. There is only one attraction I tolerate. I always go into the Fun House.

ON THE BRULE

I was eleven when my Aunt Evelyn took me on the Burlington Northern train from Chicago to Superior, Wisconsin, where I was to spend the summer with my Uncle Mac and my Aunt Lena.

Lena was Evelyn and my mother's younger sister. The three women had grown up in Northern Wisconsin, with their four brothers, children of a Swedish couple, Sven and Johanna Stephenson. The Stephensons had immigrated to Wisconsin from a small town near Stockholm in the early Twentieth Century and all but one of their children had been born in America.

My grandparents died before I was born but I had uncles, aunts, and cousins by the dozens. Only Evelyn and my mother had left Wisconsin for the big city; the rest of the family were tight-knit and harmonious in the frost-bound North.

That train ride, the longest I had ever taken, was memorable as my introduction to a miraculous new delight, the shrimp cocktail, served over ice and devoured in the club car as rich Wisconsin farm land flashed by. Eating something called a "cocktail" made me feel very grown up and sophisticated.

Uncle Mac was an engineer on the Great Northern Railway out of Superior, Wisconsin. That summer in 1954, steam locomotives were being phased out in favor of the new streamlined diesel engines like those that pulled the

Empire Builder with its sleek domed observation cars from Chicago to Seattle and Portland. Mac still piloted old Number 818, a giant iron behemoth of a steam driven switcher with its eight huge drive wheels and boxy tender.

Dense billows of smoke smelling sweetly of coal dust, hot oil and water vapor filled the air above this blackened metal monster as it pushed and pulled steel and wooden boxcars through the switch yard. My cousins, Terry and Timmy and I would sneak into the yards and climb a signal gantry which spanned tracks we knew Uncle Mac would take on his return to the round house. Seeing us hanging precariously overhead, my uncle would cause Number 818 to belch acrid clouds of steam and smoke which covered us in grit and grim and insured that the wrath of Aunt Lena would be upon us later that afternoon.

Saturday nights Uncle Mac took us to the stock car races to see my second cousin Lenny drive in the demolition derby. Lenny coveted Uncle Mac's car, a 1952 Hudson Hornet, with its dual single-barreled carburetors, dual-intake manifold, and powerful straight-six engine, perfect for racing, but Mac knew better than to let Lenny near what served as the family car. Mac would blast music from the radio and keep a beat alternately using the gas pedal and then the brake as he drove us to the dirt track at the Douglas County Fair grounds.

In the derby, Lenny drove an old Plymouth Coupe with no windows and the number thirteen painted in bright orange paint on the door. Its sides creased and dented and spattered with mud from the wet track, it burned oil and its headlights were broken out. The object of the derby was to destroy all competitors by crashing ruthlessly into them. Lenny's winning technique was to smash backwards into the other cars so that his engine wasn't damaged from the crash. The last car still running was the winner. One night he brought home first prize, a re-purposed football trophy, the words, "Grand Champion," lettered in ball point pen on masking tape across its corroded front.

Terry and Timmy shared a room upstairs in their parents' turn of the century frame house. Not a large room, it had a dormer overlooking the street in which Terry had assembled his HO gauge train set. HO was a new, smaller sized, more realistically detailed version of electric model train, definitely more elegant than the clunky O gauge American Flier set I had at home. Colorful boxcars sported logos for the Union Pacific Railroad, The Atchison, Topeka and Santa Fe Railway, The Canadian National, The Burlington Northern, The Soo Line and, of course, The Great Northern. There was a stock steam engine and tender upon which Terry had glued a Great Northern trademark cut from a train schedule.

My cousins had bunk beds and I was to sleep on an old mattress dragged out into the middle of the room. While they climbed into pajamas decorated with images of cowboys shooting Indians, riding horses, and roping steers, I was content in my skivvies, never having liked the feel of flannel against my skin.

"Aunt Evelyn is going home tomorrow," Timmy said, "But you're staying?"

Did I detect a hint of animosity in his question? "Uh huh. I'm here for the summer."

"Keen!" Said Terry. "Let's ask Pop if we can go to Uncle Rick's."

Terry was my age and two years older than Timmy. He was clearly excited to have a companion for the next month. Timmy must have felt a bit left out although we tried to involve him in all our activities. Said activities included wrestling matches during which the two larger boned, heavier set brothers both could pin skinny me to the floor with little effort.

But the quintessential summer adventure was a visit to Uncle Rick's cabin on the Brule River. Uncle Rick was the brother closest to my mother's age and her favorite among the siblings. Her stories of growing up teased and tormented by the older boys, then rescued by Rick who would vex them right back are still vivid in my memory.

The Brule River, famous for fly fishing, cascaded over rocks and ledges as it fell northward to empty into Lake Superior. Its clear, cold water was home to Brook, Brown and Rainbow Trout and the migration paths of Coho and Chinook salmon. Uncle Rick's place was up a short rise from the river bed, surrounded by stately pines and tall cedars. In spring, wildflowers dotted a clearing downriver from the cabin and in summer, young eagles circled overhead, patrolling the river banks. Occasionally, someone braved the rapids in a canoe, but mostly this cool, pristine paradise was peopled only by a few fly fishermen. And their nephews.

The interior of Uncle Rick's cabin was pine paneled and sparse, with a large central table piled with fishing gear. We watched fascinated while Uncle Rick tied a fly, explaining the intricacies to us as he wrapped and wound colored thread or feathers around a fish hook held tightly in a miniature vise.

"This one's a Blue Winged Olive," he'd say, "Good for early spring. This other one's a Yellow Sally, good for summer. Trout like these Stone Fly Larva, but the weather has to be just right." If I could remember all this stuff I might make a good fly fisherman someday. And if I didn't catch the hook in my backside, which happened once or twice.

That summer Uncle Rick attempted to teach me to fly cast. Donning waders, he stood in the shallows along the edge of the river where water-logged branches had clumped creating sheltering pools from the raging currents of the Brule. "Now, watch!," he called. Placing his line in the water in front of him he slowly lifted his rod vertically and tipped it slightly behind his shoulders. With a quick forward stroke and a twist of his wrist he brought the tip of his rod down pointing horizontally up stream. In a graceful arc, the line rolled, looped, and straightened out before striking the water. After a few more demonstrations I heard him yell, as I was afraid he would, "Now you try it!"

I stood uneasy on slippery rocks, the cold water lapping contemptuously at my rubber boots. The rod felt heavy and unbalanced and the line seemed to be everywhere but where I wanted it to be. I swung the rod back overhead but the line snagged on a log. On my second attempt I managed to place the fly a few feet in front of me, certainly an improvement! After a while, although awkward and self-conscious, I began to get the hang of it. Soon I was placing my fly well out into the stream and only occasionally feeling the sting of the line against my arm or neck. I was a fly fisherman! Of course, it helps if you can also catch fish.

Uncle Rick's quota of Steelheads and Brook Trout were circling lethargically in a bucket of water. Later he would swiftly cut through their necks with his stag-horn handled buck knife, gut and scrape them clean of scales and fry them with salt and pepper in butter for our dinner. A neighbor's golden retriever would arrive to requisition the fish heads and we would lather up with 6-12 mosquito repellent and settle down in creaking old Adirondack chairs to read comic books. The evening air was always cool and the sound of hoot owls mingled with the croaking of unseen frogs and the irreverent chirping of crickets.

The following day we ran wild in the woods where Ojibwa, Cree and Potawatomi once hunted beaver and elk. Snatches of Longfellow's "Song of Hiawatha" surfaced in vague memory and any minute I expected to come upon the wigwam of old Nokomis and the shores of Gitche Gumee.

We'd settled on a game of hide-and-go-seek with Timmy as "it." Terry and I scampered into the tall pines and aspens to await the inevitable, "olly olly, oxen free," calling us back to home base, positive that Timmy would never find us. The sun shone brightly through the aspen leaves and large rain drops fell sporadically onto the sandy ground, scattering tiny tree frogs that were the size of one's thumb. When it rains while the sun shines, I thought, that means the devil is beating his wife. This bit of arcane wisdom undoubtedly came from one of my many uncles.

What began as random dollops escalated into a shimmering silver curtain of rain lit incongruously by the errant summer sun. Up was down; right was left; forward became backward. I was disoriented and, not knowing which way to turn, began to run. I ran as if speed alone would lessen the impact of that pummeling torrent. The tears of the devil's wife mixed with my own and I gasped for breath, wondering if it were possible to drown on land.

Minutes seemed like hours as I plummeted down what might have been a road or a clearing in that impenetrable forest veiled in rainstorm. Ahead of me a blankness congealed, grew denser and darker than the luminous deluge. It thickened and became solid. A house! A log cabin, not my uncle's, but welcome indeed!

Or so I thought. My cousins had filled me with North

Woods lore of fantastic dimensions. Besides the requisite ghosts, goblins, and spirits of dead Indians, there were the so called "real people" who you didn't want to meet on a dark night, or even on a rainy day. One such real person was old Mr. Carver, who was at worst, an ogre, and at best, a curmudgeon. He lived down river in an old log cabin not unlike the one I was standing in front of, where, according to my cousins, he had done away with his young wife but kept her decaying body in a back room and attempted to feed her grapes. I never quite understood about the grapes, but I was willing to be very much afraid of Mr. Carver. I was about to venture back up the road when the door suddenly opened and a firm hand gripped my arm pulling me haphazardly into the cabin.

Mr. Carver, if this was indeed he, was an imposing presence. A large man, he towered above me. With unruly hair and bristling beard, his immense form seemed to fill the room, choking out the light.

"Don't you know enough to come in out of the rain, boy?"

"No, Sir. I mean, yes, Sir," I stammered.

"Well, sit down. I'll get you a towel or a blanket or something."

The something turned out to be an old gray army blanket that smelled of moth balls, but it was dry and I was shivering as much from the cold as from my fear that I might soon be flayed and roasted like a Steelhead Trout or stuffed with grapes and kept forever in some dark room. I slouched down on an antique rocker while my host eased into a threadbare arm chair so overstuffed it seemed to swallow him, large as he was.

"You visiting up at Rick Stephenson's?"

"Yes I am, Sir. He's my uncle."

"Hmpf. Catchin' any fish?"

"I'm just learning."

"People are goin' to fish this river out one of these days. They got no sense. Damn fools!"

"I hope not, Sir."

"I'm all for humanity. I just don't like people very much."

"Why don't you like people, Mr. Carver?"

"Is that your wife," I asked, instantly aware I may have foolishly conjured a doleful memory.

"Yes," he said, "That's Aiko. Gone now, five years." His eyes seemed to glaze, then narrowed, hardened. He became still and seemed to drift into some private place to which I was denied entry. I had to know.

"What happened?"

Reverie interrupted, he focused his scowl on my still shivering self. Moments passed, then he exhaled long and low, more like a whisper than a gush. Although my body was shaking, my mind was paralyzed. I was afraid of what I might hear yet I could not avert mindful attention. He must have sensed my disquiet but overlooked, or chose to overlook my morbid curiosity, because his glare softened and he gave a subtle nod.

"You probably think I'm an old coot, but I'm only 42. I was in the war, in the South Pacific for most of it. We sailed into Sagami Bay at Tokyo near the end of the war, but that's neither here nor there. Truman dropped the bombs and it was over; we came home.

"That's when I met Aiko. Christmas, 1945. I was waiting to be discharged up in Sacramento. They had these internment camps full of Japanese. They were mostly Americans but I guess they wanted to believe they were all spies. Whole families were displaced. When they started closing down the camps in '45 they'd give them each $25 and a train ticket home.

"I was assigned to process the detainees that were still being held at this migrant workers' camp. Aiko's parents decided to emigrate to Japan. Aiko wanted to stay but no longer had a home to return to. There was something about her sad, dark eyes and, well, it was Christmas, so I took her out of the camp and placed her in a hotel in town. I had to sneak her into the place because anti-Japanese sentiment was still very strong. She was just a young girl, just 16, but I was afraid for her, afraid of the violence that might be directed toward her because of her race.

"I wangled a three-day pass and spent the entire time with Aiko. She told me about living in the camp. Concentration camps is what they were! Most people didn't know about them...still don't. But on the West Coast anyone of Japanese ancestry was excluded from the area, and that meant something like 120,000 people!

"Thousands were relocated and interned. Aiko and her family were pulled from their home which they subsequently lost along with most of their possessions. They were waiting in Sacramento to be transferred to Texas, Wyoming, or maybe even New Mexico where conditions would be even worse. It was overcrowded, there were no private cooking facilities or toilets and they were surrounded by barbed wire and armed guards. Aiko remembered hearing of a detainee who was shot for leaving the compound. They had a feeling of absolute helplessness.

"Once I was discharged we decided to get married. Aiko was underage so we lied about her age, got the license, the blood tests and found a local judge who was reluctant, but overcame his prejudice long enough to marry us. We looked for work all across the country: Salt Lake City, Denver, Kansas City, but had little luck. We encountered prejudice everywhere we went. We'd be asked to leave restaurants, be given dirty looks on the street as we walked, hand and hand. But we had each other. Finally we came to Milwaukee where a navy buddy of mine had said there were jobs at the Schlitz brewery."

He paused, knocked the ashes from his pipe into an ashtray. With a profound look asked, "How old are you, boy?"

"I'm eleven," I answered.

"So how can I explain the joys of marriage to an eleven year old?"

"I understand lots of stuff," I replied. In reality, I understood practically nothing but I wasn't about to admit it.

"All you need to know," he began, "is that we were totally, completely in love. We were soul mates, inseparable, like we were one person in two bodies. She was so lovely, so quiet, so small. When she smiled it was like sunshine on a cloudless day. Her voice was musical, like tiny bells ringing. I loved the way her fine dark hair fell across her shoulders and down her back. I couldn't bare it when she was ill treated. But we persevered.

"The Schlitz brewery in Milwaukee was on Galena

Street. A huge place! I heard they were beginning to hire Negros for the first time so I thought, why not a Japanese American? They had machines that actually loaded the bottles into boxes but they still needed people to schlep them around.

"I could get a job, that was OK for me, but I asked if there was something for my wife. Something in the office, maybe? Oh, and I should mention that she's Japanese American? I emphasized the word, 'American'. Now, Milwaukee was full of the families of German emigrants. Joseph Schlitz was from Germany. The Uihleins that ran the place were from Germany. Many of the workers there were of German decent. And guess who we had just fought a war with? Germany! But they wouldn't hire Aiko.

"Two years later, I'd saved a little money working double shifts at Schlitz and I wanted to try something different. I'd heard there were wealthy people from Chicago and even some politicians from Washington who were buying places up north or staying at fishing lodges. We found a cheap spot of land here along the Brule and built this cabin. I became a tour guide for fly fishermen and I've been doing that ever since. We lived a nice peaceful life here. Never any trouble from ignorant people. It was like finding the end of the rainbow for us. It was paradise on earth."

Again the man paused in his story, his eyes acquiring a sudden sadness that shook me. He turned to the window. "It's stopped raining. I'll walk you back to your uncle's."

"Wait," I said. "What happened to her, to Aiko?"

"She walked out to the hard road to get the mail one morning. She took Oscar, our collie with her. Oscar ran out across the highway. She ran after him. A semi plowed into her. He couldn't stop in time. Knocked her 40 feet. She died instantly. When Oscar came home, I shot him."

I never told my cousins the true story of Mr. Carver. I guess the story of the grapes was more to their liking, anyway. A few days later, Uncle Mac came to get us in the Hudson. The radio was playing a new song by a man with a strange name. We laughed at it: "Elvis Presley? What kind of a name was that?"

When it was time for me to return home I was allowed

to ride the train alone. I immediately went to the club car. I sat there, counting out my change to see if I had enough for a shrimp cocktail. Tall pines sweeping by outside the window gave way to oaks and maples. I thought about Aiko and Mr. Carver. I wondered at the war I was too young to remember and at the life of a fisherman who had fought long and hard for contentment, only to have it taken from him in a senseless accident. I was glad for my family, for my many uncles and cousins, and that there would never be another war like that one. Little did I know.

GIANTS IN THE EARTH

There Were Giants in the Earth in Those Days
——Genesis 6:4

In 1870, in Potosi, Wisconsin, workers digging the foundation for a saw mill near the banks of the Mississippi River unearthed two skeletons. One measured eight feet in length and the other measured seven and one half feet in length. Their skulls had high cheek bones and double sets of teeth. The skeletons were surrounded by arrowheads and strange, toy-like objects.

In 1897, at Maple Creek, Wisconsin, three burial mounds were excavated. A skeleton measuring nine feet was uncovered. With it were found copper rods and other relics. Sometime later, at West Bend, Wisconsin, near the Lizard Creek County Park, a skeleton of approximately eight feet in height was assembled and displayed. These discoveries were reported by the newspapers.

There were reports of other skeletons being found ranging from seven to ten feet with large skulls, double rows of teeth, six fingers and toes. Their heads were said to be elongated and their nasal features pointed. Strange as it may seem, none of these fantastic skeletons ever appeared at the Smithsonian or at any other reputable scientific venue. There were rumors of a cover-up.

Of course there were fakes. P. T. Barnum had his

version of the Cardiff Giant. It was, however, a fake replica of...a fake. The original had been manufactured by George Hull, a cigar maker from Baraboo, Wisconsin.

Hull bought a twelve foot piece of gypsum from a quarry in Fort Dodge, Iowa, and shipped it to Chicago, where he hired a German stonecutter named Edward Salle to carve it into the figure of a giant Stone Age man. The details were extraordinary, right down to the pores of the skin. Hull shipped the giant to his cousin's farm in New York State, near the village of Cardiff. He then buried his creation and arranged for it to be "discovered" over two years later, allowing the earth to naturally age the statue, so he could claim it to have been "petrified."

Hull had a great deal of success exhibiting the Cardiff Giant—so much so that P. T. Barnum knew he had to acquire it for his museum of freaks and oddities. Hull wouldn't sell the giant however, so Barnum commissioned his own sculpture. The Barnum version was promoted as the "real" Cardiff Giant, discrediting Hull's. "The public," said P. T. Barnum, "likes to be humbugged."

Beloit College, Beloit, Wisconsin, April, 1912

Paul Peterson was young for an Assistant Professor of Archeology: only thirty-four. His rapid advance through the faculty of Beloit College was due to the fact that he was one of the foremost experts in his field of Native American Studies and had amassed a sizeable collection of Indian artifacts, including arrowheads, cooking implements, and old bones, for the college's Natural History Museum.

The front row in his lecture hall was always filled with young women. In fact, his class roster often showed a female majority, due less to the subject matter than to his striking good looks. Today he was finishing a unit on the Mound Builders of the Midwestern states. On the blackboard behind him he had sketched the shapes of some of the mounds found near Lake Mendota near Madison, Wisconsin.

"As you can see, some resemble human torsos and others appear to represent animals. It is possible that some of the mounds in the effigy groups had astrological alignments, which suggests that the early mound builders used them in some sort of ceremonial way.

"There really is no doubt that the mounds were built by the ancestors of the Native American tribes living in the area. It has taken years for science to debunk the 'Lost Tribes' theory that was prevalent in the last century. No, it was not the Israelites, the Aztecs, the Vikings, the Greeks or the Egyptians that built the earthworks. More likely it was the Ho-Chunk or the Oneota or the Potawatomie. The fact that Native Americans no longer build mounds is one of the weakest of arguments. After all, the Egyptians no longer build pyramids.

"This spring I will be taking a research group to Delavan where some two hundred mounds have been discovered. I have obtained a grant to excavate and hope to make some interesting discoveries. Some of you advanced students may wish to apply as interns. And now, I believe the class is over, or else my watch is fast."

Ellen Ewing remained seated until the classroom was emptied of students. Professor Peterson was struggling with a stack of papers that resisted being crammed into his briefcase. "Here, Professor Peterson," she said, "let me help you with that."

Ellen was not one of Peterson's star pupils. She made decent marks on exams but her term papers lacked insight. She was one of the front row girls, prone to dressing in shorter skirts than propriety required and in the habit of twirling a pin curl on her finger during Peterson's lectures. Peterson had noticed her, all right, and being aware of the precarious position a faculty member occupied, was disinclined to encourage the girl.

"Professor," Ellen said, moving closer, "I think I could be quite helpful to you on that excavation you mentioned."

"Ellen, I appreciate your interest, but there are students here who have invested more time and effort to the study of archeology than you have. To be honest, you haven't applied yourself very much this term. Not to archeology, that is."

"But Professor Peterson, I'm related to the owners of Lake Lawn. Anna Phillips is my father's cousin. Lake Lawn is where those Indian mounds are, isn't it? Her sons run the hotel there and I happen to know they've dug around their land looking for arrowheads and such. I could put in a good word."

Peterson knew that Ellen Ewing could just as well put in a bad word. Her flirtation was annoying, but common sense told him she had a point. The local farmers around Delavan weren't happy when academic types starting digging up their fields. And Lake Lawn had perhaps one hundred of the mounds he was interested in. He needed the owners' permission and cooperation if the dig was to be successful.

"You know, Ellen, I think the experience of field work might be just the thing to get you on track with your studies. I hope you have a good pair of overalls."

Circus Winter Quarters, Delavan, Wisconsin, 1864

There wasn't much for a giant to do in a side show. Even those working for P. T. Barnum at his museum in New York were bored most of the time. Oh, they stood in front of crowds, told their life stories (usually fabricated), and sold postcards and photos of themselves. In a circus, however, you had to have a skill.

You could be a strong man—but who would believe a giant *wasn't* strong? You could do tricks riding a horse— but very few circus horses could support the weight of a four hundred pound man. Maybe you could juggle dwarves. Or wrestle alligators. There must be something a giant could do!

Barnabas Kovacs could have been billed as the largest man in the world. He was seven feet eight inches in height. He measured fifty-nine inches around the chest. The calf of his leg measured twenty-two inches in diameter, his arm nineteen inches, and the span from the tip of his thumb to the end of his fingers was thirteen and one half inches. He weighed four hundred and twelve pounds. He was a large man.

Kovacs had worked briefly for P. T. Barnum in New York as a "curiosity" but had tired of being on exhibition: the leers, the jeers, the perpetual sense of being an outsider had grated on him. He traveled to the Midwest to join the Mabie Brothers' Circus, signing on as...well, as a giant...

and now found himself in Delavan, Wisconsin, as the circus returned to its winter quarters to await the spring season.

The circus' sideshow manager, Harry Buckley, suggested to Barnabas that he learn trick riding. Buckley had begun his own career as a stunt rider at the age of twelve. As Buckley was himself over six feet tall he felt that Kovacs' great height and weight would not be a problem if the right horse was used. He would be a sensation, he told the giant. Barnabas Kovacs was not so sure.

The first trial of the giant's equestrian ability took place in the practice barn one crisp November afternoon. The principle trainer, Eric Sorensen, had brought the stallion, Goliath, into the ring for Barnabas to ride. Goliath was a giant in his own right: he stood nineteen hands high and weighted over two thousand pounds. He had been a draft horse, pulling wagons, and so was not used to riders. When Barnabas tried mounting him, he bulked. Barnabas tried again and this time landed on the soft sawdust with a heavy thud.

"This is not going the work," Barnabas complained.

"I wish we could use one of the trick horses, but I'm afraid you're too big. Say, I know just the thing! Two horses. You could straddle them and your weight would be distributed evenly."

"Straddle them? You're kidding me, aren't you?"

"It'll look great. You'll dwarf the horses."

"Eric, I've never even been on a horse before. I can't do it." Barnabas left the barn, dejected and cursing his size. Was he doomed to always be on the sidelines, watching others perform? Was he only suitable to be presented as a freak of nature? He wanted more.

Eric had persevered with Barnabas' training, starting him off driving a chariot pulled by two horses. Barnabas then practiced standing with one foot on each animal's back while they remained stationary in the stall. He was beginning to find his sense of balance and the animals were getting used to his huge bulk. Gradually, the impossible pyramid of horses and giant ventured out into the ring, walking at first, then trotting. Barnabas fell a few times, but eventually the act began to take shape.

By spring Barnabas Kovacs was a full-fledged trick rider. He was looking forward to joining the company for the year's grand tour. He would be a star and yet, he felt alone, isolated. It seemed always to have been that way.

Barnabas had been born in 1839 in Zanesville, Ohio. His father was a farmer, a tall man, nearing six feet in height, and his mother was of medium build. He had two brothers and a sister, all whom were of normal size. Barnabas started to grow larger than his siblings at an early age: by age six he was as tall as his mother and by age fifteen he had reached six feet two inches, and was taller than his father. His unique proportions set him apart from his schoolmates and often provoked the natural meanness of the other children.

After high school, Barnabas worked on his father's farm. He continued to grow and until he towered well over seven feet. It was then that he came to the attention of Phineas Taylor Barnum, who's American Museum in New York City featured oddities as well as live acts. Barnum had one of the smallest people in the world, General Tom Thumb, who stood at two feet, eleven inches. Barnum lured Barnabas to New York and soon was showing him as the Zanesville Giant, positioning him next to Tom Thumb for contrast.

At the museum, Barnabas met Melana Kasprzak. Melana was seven feet five and one half inches tall. She had a pleasant, oval face with symmetrical features and her body was slim and well proportioned. Barnabas fell for her at once. They began a romantic relationship that didn't remain unnoticed by Barnum. He suggested they be married at the museum. He would sell tickets. There was something about the vulgar commercialism of this idea that cooled their romance and threatened to extinguish its flame. They began to drift apart. Then Barnabas left for the circus.

The following year, while Barnabas was learning to ride, there was a fire at Barnum's American Museum. It was the peak of the Civil War and P. T. Barnum was as pro-Union as any Northerner could be. He had taken Commodore Nutt, a midget barely taller than Tom Thumb, to visit President Abraham Lincoln in the White House to express his support. He had hired an actress who had spied for the

Union to lecture about her adventures and he had produced many other pro-Unionist exhibits. The result was that a Confederate arsonist set his building ablaze.

Melana Kasprzak was trapped on the third floor. The stairwells were filled with smoke and flames consumed the wooden risers. She ran to the window, but was too large to fit through it. She was beginning to panic and flailed her arms at men who had come to lead her out of the building, knocking them over. It looked as though Melana would become a casualty of the fire.

Someone noticed a derrick standing nearby. It was immediately put into service to save the giantess. The men managed to break out the wall surrounding a window to make an opening large enough for her huge form. It took eighteen men, but Melana was finally lowered by block and tackle to the street. She weighted three hundred and eighty-two pounds.

Barnabas had written to Melana, telling her of his experiences in the circus. "Come join me here," he wrote. "These people are kind and eager to teach you things. I've learned trick horseback riding. You could do it too!" As the museum was a total loss, Melana now had no home. Barnum wanted to send her on a tour of Europe which didn't interest her. Did she still have feelings for Barnabas Kovacs? It was possible. She arrived in Delavan in early 1865 only to learn that Jeremiah Mabie was closing down his circus. Both she and Barnabas were now out of a job.

Lake Lawn Farm, Delavan, Wisconsin, May, 1912

Ernest and Jeremiah Mabie had brought their circus, the U. S. Olympic Circus, from New York to rural Wisconsin, in 1847, purchasing four hundred acres of farm land on the shores of Lake Delavan. Circuses hadn't yet hit upon the idea of traveling by train—this would be an innovation born in Delavan some thirty years later—so their range of mobility was limited by horse and wagon technology. They decided on Southern Wisconsin, central to the Midwestern states, as the ideal place to settle in for the winter. It was the beginnings of "Circus Town, U.S.A." as Delavan would come to be called, where over the years, twenty-six different circuses had found a home or had been originated. Among those circuses born in Delavan was Barnum and Bailey's Greatest Show on Earth.

In 1878, Anna Mary Phillips, then the widow of Jeremiah Mabie, resided at the Mabie farm, the former winter quarters of the Mabie circus. She had named it Lake Lawn and opened a guest house there which could accommodate fifty people, and as many horses. Lake Lawn Hotel soon became a destination for vacationers from Chicago and Milwaukee. There were expansions and additions including a grand dining hall, a ballroom and a bathing beach.

By 1912, the circuses had left Delavan, closing down, consolidating or moving to warmer locations. The brothers Ernest and Chester Phillips, the sons of Mary Phillips, had taken over directorship of the hotel and resort. They were astute businessmen and also amateur archeologists. As late as 1836 there had been an encampment of Potawatomi along the shores of Lake Delavan. The Phillips brothers searched for arrowheads and other artifacts and found thousands of small items, apparently modern in origin.

Then they learned about the Mound Builders: ancient Woodlands Peoples that had lived in large communities all over the state of Wisconsin between 800 and 1200 AD. These early inhabitants left behind thousands of earthen mounds of various sizes and shapes that often contained burials. The Phillips brothers were able to identify several sites where what appeared to be low hills were in fact constructions whose circumferences traced the outlines of birds, animals or strange creatures: effigy mounds.

Ernest Phillips entered the common room at the Lake Lawn Hotel. A young man was perusing the glass case containing part of the collection of arrowheads and pottery shards he and his brother had on display for hotel guests. "I'm particularly proud of that one," he told the man. "Very old flint knife."

"No, actually, it's modern," said Paul Peterson. "Potawatomie, I would guess. No more than fifteen, twenty years old. This pot shard here, though...that's quite interesting."

"My brother thinks it's just from an old flower pot. From the circus days. I like it though. Nice texturing to the design."

"I'd place that piece around 1100 AD. See how the pattern curves as if it represents water? There was probably some contact between the people who made this and one of the Mississippian cultures."

"You sound like you know what you're talking about."

"I should hope so. Paul Peterson, Professor of Archeology, Beloit College," the man said, offering his hand.

"I'm Ernest Phillips, manager of the hotel. I'm sort of an archeologist myself. Collected all these and lots more."

"I hope you aren't digging up any sites that should be excavated using proper scientific methods. Arrowhead hunting can be very damaging, you know. There is so much we can learn from the juxtaposition of artifacts. Many minute details you may be overlooking. A single kernel of corn could tell volumes about their lifestyle."

Phillips thought this condescending professor fellow was rude and insulting. Damaging the sites? What a nerve! Phillips knew what he was doing. He was careful. Always put the dirt back. He even kept a record of where the best mounds were. It was his family's land, after all...well, his family's and their neighbor's. He'd recently been over to the Tilden's farm. Discovered three big mounds there. Probably not a good idea to mention those to this professor. Keep them for himself.

"I think I've a relative of yours with my party," Peterson said. "A student of mine named Ellen Ewing. Says your mother is her father's cousin."

"Ewing? Ewing? No, I don't recall anyone related to us by that name. The name though...wait a minute...I think I remember a little gal by that name that worked here last summer. Yes. I think that's the one. She was a maid. Not a very good one as I recall. Light brown hair? Very giggly?"

"I see. Well, I suppose she exaggerated her relationship to you to get a place on my research staff."

"You're not just here for a vacation then?"

"We hope to do some digging. It would be a great help to us," Peterson told Phillips, realizing that good politics was a first principle of good scientific research, "if you could lend a hand. Your expertise and knowledge of the local sites..."

"Yes, of course. I'd be delighted." And I can keep an eye on you, thought Phillips. An eagle eye.

Paul Peterson couldn't sleep. The day had started out well, with the Phillips brothers giving him and his students a tour of the mounds on the Lake Lawn property. However, there was something lacking about what they had been shown: these were small, cone-shaped mounds, not the spectacular effigy configurations Peterson had expected. Was he being misdirected? He thought it was a possibility.

The room at Lake Lawn Hotel was comfortable, the sheets clean and a goose-down comforter lay folded at the foot of the bed in case the cool night air that breezed through his open window turned to a chill. Still, he lay in the darkness consumed by worry. He didn't wish to antagonize his hosts, yet he was certain better sites were close by. What to do?

The door opened and closed silently, momentarily allowing a gentle wind to waft across the restless sleeper, as though the room were taking a deep breath, then holding it in anticipation. Sheets rustled and pulled away from him. A sudden warmth pressed against him. With the automatic logic of half-sleep, Peterson rolled toward the soft form, encircled it in his arms, breathed with the deepness of a contented dreamer.

Her hands explored him. Her mouth found his. Then the pleasant descent into dreamland found its limit. Peterson strained to awake, like a drowning swimmer struggling for the surface of a choppy sea. Curiously, he found he was already awake. The sweet fragrance of the naked body of Ellen Ewing reached his nostrils just as this bizarre revelation reached his incredulous mind.

He pictured himself standing before the tenure committee at the college, receiving his walking papers: conduct unbecoming– breach of ethics– debauchery– disgraceful behavior! How could he face his parents, his friends? Throwing away years of hard work and devotion to his study of ancient peoples. He would never be able to work for an educational institution again.

But only if he was found out. Ellen. Tender, delectable,

ambrosial, sumptuous, intoxicating Ellen. He surrendered to his desires and she carried him on a wave back into the dream where he need not be Professor Paul Peterson, dedicated archeologist and scholar, mentor of young minds. At that crucial and ecstatic moment when he crossed from dream to undreamable, he thought he felt a physical click inside of his brain.

They lay, exhausted on the damp sheets. He brushed nervous fingers through her hair. "You lied to me, you know," he told her. "You lied about being related to the Phillips family."

"Paul, darling," she answered, perhaps a little too sweet and demurring, "I just had to be with you. You aren't mad, are you?"

"Mad? No. Disappointed. And I was counting on your influence with the Phillips brothers."

"They didn't show you the best mounds. I know where better ones are. I worked here last summer, you know."

"You know, I think you're about to redeem yourself,' said Peterson as he rolled on top of her.

Delavan, Wisconsin, summer, 1865

Melana and Barnabas had been married on April 14th, the same day that Abraham Lincoln was assassinated. A black mood enveloped the country, finding its way to Delavan. It arrived at the same time a large flock of crows descended on the town, emigrants from the fields of carrion back east.

The two giants spent their wedding night in a cozy room at the Park Hotel downtown. Their lovemaking disturbed the other guests and broke the bed; they were asked to leave. Returning to the circus colony on the Mabie's farm they found that a meeting of all circus personnel had been called. Jeremiah Mabie had announced that he was disbanding the circus. He had had enough.

The war years had been rough on the circuses. Located mostly in the North and the East, they had lost their southern territories. The Mabie circus had started to tour in a more westerly direction: Iowa, Minnesota and Nebraska. The roads were bad, the population sparse and scattered and the weather abominable. Only in the largest towns was it profitable to stay for more than a day. In Council Bluffs, Iowa, a fierce storm destroyed the main tent. A replacement took many weeks to arrive. Mabie packed up and returned to Wisconsin.

Barnabas went to Harry Buckley, the man who had encouraged him to learn to ride. Buckley had been the Mabie's principle rider and had later organized his own circus, touring the Southern United States, Nassau, Haiti and Jamaica before returning to Delavan some five years ago. If there were anything to know about the circus business, Buckley knew it. But Buckley only talked about starting some new business in Delavan: perhaps a livery, a hardware store, or a cheese factory.

Some of the performers and roustabouts had found positions with other circuses. But these were small venues and employment was limited by budgets that didn't include sideshow personnel. No one wanted to hire a giant—much less a pair of giants. Barnabas turned to the townspeople of Delavan, Wisconsin, for help.

It was then that the giant discovered just how much animosity the locals had for circus people. Oh, there were businessmen who had invested in circuses, hotel owners who depended on the circus trade, a saloon or two that survived on the inevitable propensity toward inebriation of circus folk, but "Circus Town, U.S.A." saw the circuses as a necessary evil—with emphasis on the word, evil. No one hired giants.

Circumstances became more and more dire for Barnabas and his bride. Mabie had allowed some of his former employees to camp on his land while he sold off wagons and livestock. Helping out, the giants earned barely enough money to survive the summer while living in a tent near the lake. Then Melana got sick. It started as a bad cough and a cold that would not subside. Her breathing became difficult and it was apparent that Melana had pneumonia. She died in Barnabas' arms that fall.

Tragedy heaped upon tragedy. The cemetery officials in Delavan would not allow the giantess to be buried in the town cemetery. Again Jeremiah Mabie came to the rescue. There was some hilly land to the west of his farm, he told

Barnabas, where a simple grave could be dug. Away from the house and grounds, of course. The giant was free to borrow a wagon to transport his wife to her final resting place.

Barnabas made a quick trip into town to buy flowers and a bottle of rat poison. He dug a grave on the side of a small hill with a view of the lake. Carefully, he placed Melana's body into the grave and covered it with the flowers. Crows sat on the branches of nearby cottonwoods, cackling and rustling their shiny black feathers.

The giant had made the hole wide enough for two. He slid in beside Melana and uncorked the bottle of poison. Drinking deeply, he lay back and closed his eyes. A brisk wind came up seemingly from nowhere, and began to push the loose dirt back into the grave.

Lake Lawn Farm, Delavan, Wisconsin, May, 1912

Peterson directed the students to stretch a string between two stakes so that it ran across the center of the mound. Following the path of the string, they then began to dig a narrow and shallow trench, bisecting the excavation site. The trench would allow them to examine the strata within the mound without totally destroying it. The chances were that a sampling of artifacts collected this way would indicate the use of the mound by its builders.

Ellen Ewing had led Peterson to the site earlier that morning, before the Phillips brothers were around to distract them. Now the entire research team was busy removing soil in spoonful-sized chunks, slowly and methodically. The Phillips brothers stood watching from a short distance. They were amazed that these young people could exercise such meticulous caution—and endure such tedious drudgery.

Ellen was crying softly, trying not to let it show. Paul Peterson had taken her aside and was talking to her in a low, but stern voice. "Please don't misinterpret my intentions," he said. "You're a lovely girl—pretty, sensual, exciting. But I can't have the others know about us. Don't you see how dangerous that is? I could lose my job! Just for a fling!"

Just for a fling. It stung her, hurt her terribly. She sniffed back some tears, clenched her teeth and forced a smile to her lips. "Yes, Professor Peterson," she said. "I understand. I'll be good." She turned and tried not to run as she left the dig site.

Peterson watched her go. He was about to follow when the cry came: "Skull! There's a skull here!"

"Okay, everybody stop what they're doing," Peterson said. He stooped to examine the bit of dull white bone that was now exposed in the trench. Carefully, he brushed around it, becoming more excited as he saw the extent of it.

"Look at the size of that!" he exclaimed once the skull was uncovered.

"Over here," said a student. "Here's another one."

"Take it slowly now. Make sketches of the placements. We should excavate the entire skeletons in the next few days. My God! They look huge!"

Peterson thought to himself that here was either an amazing scientific discovery, or a career-destroyer. When things didn't fit the theory in science, you either changed the theory—or you ignored the evidence. It didn't always depend upon the facts—more often than not it depended upon the rank of the individual making the discovery. In Peterson's case, he would probably be laughed at, ridiculed. Better take it slow and easy.

The Phillips brothers, however, had no intention of taking it slow and easy. A quick glance, one to the other, mutual nods, and they hurried off to the telephone. They told their good friend and fellow amateur archeologist, Maurice Morrissey all about the skeletons of giants they (the Phillips brothers) had just unearthed. The Lost Tribes! Maurice Morrissey was thrilled and eager to come to witness the skeletons for himself. Only he was on his way to a meeting of the Republican State Central Committee over in Madison. It would have to wait.

Morrissey didn't wait, however, before telling a reporter from the New York Times who was covering the committee meeting. He may have exaggerated somewhat. The reporter phoned in his story which appeared in the Times on the following morning. By the time Paul Peterson and his students had uncovered enough of the skeletons to discover the bits of modern clothing in the grave, the Times had reported:

...Upon opening one large mound at Lake Lawn farm, eighteen skeletons were discovered by the Phillips Brothers. The heads, presumably those of men, are much larger than the heads of any race which inhabit America to-day. From directly over the eye sockets, the head slopes straight back and the nasal bones protrude far above the cheek bones. The jaw bones are long and pointed, bearing a minute resemblance to the head of the monkey. The teeth in the front of the jaw are regular molars...

GHOST STORY

The funeral was tomorrow. There was something about not having had a chance to say goodbye that kept her awake, lying on the hard, unfamiliar mattress in her mother's guest room: a room she had once shared with her sister; a room in which the fairies and elves wallpaper had been replaced with blue roses and green vines.

The room was hot, stifling so. There seemed to be a heavy weight pressing down on her chest, making it hard to breathe. She managed a few short gasps. The mattress on which she lay was lumpy and uncomfortable. She tossed and turned, throwing the covers aside. Now on her back, she had a prickling sensation, as if myriad small insects were plucking at her skin with sharp pincers.

She forced herself to take a long, deep breath and then let the air out slowly. This calmed her somewhat, alleviating the prickling sensation. Still, sleep refused to come to her. She stared up at the ceiling. In the murky darkness her eyes began to play tricks.

An array of indistinct shapes now covered the ceiling, shifting and turning like a dance floor seen from above, but out of focus. The rotating forms began to lengthen downward, pushing swirling funnels of darkness at her. Their tendrils reached her, grabbed onto her arms and legs, encircled her neck, pulling her upwards. Abruptly, the ceiling of tornadoes vanished and she fell back on the bed.

Sweat covered her. She rolled off the mattress, set her feet upon the rug and snapped on the bedside lamp. She glanced down at the ornate pattern of the Persian style carpet. It was a modern knock-off of a antique rug, like the one at her grandmother Agnes' house. She remembered playing on her grandmother's oriental rug as a child, tracing the unfamiliar geometric patterns with a finger and imagining herself as a tiny creature traversing the colorful labyrinth.

Now, as she stood in the room, she felt weak and unsteady: a vast carpet stretched before her like a forest floor of dead leaves and debris, obscuring any path that might have existed. She took a step and instantly was surrounded by the undulating shapes of snakes, coiling and uncoiling, writhing and rolling, their scaly forms decorated with diamonds or stripes, their red tongues darting out like miniature daggers.

She would have screamed but a constriction of her throat prevented anything louder than a hiss to exit her mouth. She feared she might fall and be lost under that rippling mass. Then the snake forms began to fade, becoming nearly transparent. Suddenly it was as if the once solid floor had liquefied beneath her and an obscene ocean's depths waited to swallow her. She leaped back onto the bed and lapsed into unconsciousness.

When she awoke the gradual light of dawn was filtering through the blinds, casting shadows that moved slowly up the wall. She felt she was drowning in the grayness of the room's dim illumination. She could just make out an antique lighting fixture thick with dust on the ceiling above her. No sound came to jar her from the blankness that spread through her like a fever. No thought or memory could supplant the paralysis that now gripped her body.

She felt herself rising, leaving her body, floating slowly upward. I'm dying, she thought, and at first the idea interested her. She sensed her own inert form below, useless to her now. She wanted to fly but found she had no control over her motion.

Panic came with the sensation that she might not be able return to her mortal shell. She could not scream in this discorporate state. Yet she struggled, mentally commanding her ethereal essence downward, down toward the physical entity, the hollow form she had once occupied. She was not yet ready for that glorious journey that awaited her. Not yet, she pleaded. With a rush, feeling returned to her, penetrating each fiber, every muscle and nerve. She lay on the hard mattress, shaking off the hallucinations of last night and this morning.

At breakfast a bowl of hot oatmeal sprinkled with cinnamon and raisins revived her. She poured extra cream into her coffee, rejoicing in her renewed vitality. Her mother fussed over the stove; the woman needed to keep busy and would have made breakfast for the entire neighborhood if she could have. Her sister sat silent and solemn beside her at the metal kitchen table, munching a cold piece of toast with red jelly dripping from it like tears.

She remembered now why she had traveled those 400 miles, cramped and cold in the front seat of a friend's Volkswagen Beetle, to sit in a cheerless kitchen on a chilly November morning: the funeral! She remembered her restless night in the over-heated room, her out-of-body experience—had it happened? Or had she dreamed it? Her father's death was not the first in her immediate family, but it was unexpected, unbelievable. There were five stages of grief, she had heard. The first was denial. But something cold had closed icy fingers around her heart. No amount of disbelief could chase away the fearful emptiness she felt.

"I should be helping you do that," she called to her mother.

"No, Rose, I want to do it. Your cousins will be here any minute. I'm cooking bacon and scrambled eggs. You know how your Uncle Michael loves his scrambled eggs. And..." she rambled on and on and Rose listened politely, throwing a weak smile in the direction of her sister, Janet. Janet stared blankly into space, the jelly still dripping.

"And really, Rose," her mother went on, "you'd think they don't teach you anything in that fancy college you go to. Look at the way you come to the table in the morning...pajamas! Have some consideration for other people, can't you?"

Was the second stage anger? Rose couldn't remember. It was going to be a long, long day.

At the graveside services Rose felt strangely removed from the somber aggregation of the mourners. The cemetery was too alien a place for her to feel comfortable in grieving openly and in concert with others.

How strange the ritual seemed! The open coffin so you could say how life-like the waxen corpse looked. The closing and tightening of the lid out of sight of the family so that the reality of the death could be delayed a bit longer. The lowering of the box into the ground only after the weepers were gone—too real! Too close to home.

And all of the dead beneath her feet awaiting the trumpet call to spring back to life: it was all too absurd. Rows and rows of gray and white marble, some ostentatious, some dilapidated, some pathetically small, signifying that a life was lived, a soul was flown away as surely as the autumn leaves are blown and buffeted by chance winds—gone but not forgotten? She thought of Shelley, of the poem about Ozymandias, of that "colossal wreck" which everyman's monument to eternal life inevitably becomes.

The very first snowflakes of winter floated lazily through the air. The mourners were beginning to disperse. Rose stared absently at the coffin and the metal stand that supported it. She examined the mechanism the would soon lower the casket gracefully into the grave. Someone has a business manufacturing those things, she thought. How curious.

As Rose turned away to return to the family car she felt someone's hand on her shoulder. It was a firm and reassuring grip as if someone were trying to give her comfort. She whirled around expectantly, but no one stood behind her. No one, in fact, was anywhere near her. She suddenly felt cold and abandoned. Then, for the first time, tears came. She ran to the car.

Whitewater, Wisconsin was over 400 miles from Rose's home town of Solon Springs, a small hamlet near Superior. Rose attended the Wisconsin State College at Whitewater and boarded with an elderly couple, the Cranstons, who lived in a Victorian era house just off campus. Elliot

Cranston struck her as a sort of curmudgeon, a white-haired elf of a man, always stalking through the house poking at things and complaining. Mildred Cranston, however, seemed the perfect embodiment of a sweet old lady, a caring person quick to provide advice even though it wasn't solicited. Rose felt very much at home at the Cranston house. It was her home away from home.

So in November of 1960, when Rose returned from attending her father's funeral, Mildred fussed over her. "You poor dear, you must be devastated," she sympathized. Rose was instructed to stretch out on the old davenport in the front room while Mrs. Cranston scurried off to fetch her a cup of hot chocolate. Tired from the long drive back from Solon Springs, she complied with the elderly woman's wishes. Being pampered was a treat after the dismal drama of the funeral.

"You must take it from me, dear child," Mildred Cranston began once Rose was tucked under a quilt, "that death is not an ending. There is an afterlife. I can testify to that."

Rose, who had taken a course in comparative religions, had studied Greek mythology and had developed an interest in Eastern philosophy, had her own opinion about death: it was indeed the end. It was final. But she would endure whatever delusional prattle this sweet old lady was about to deliver because...well, because she was a sweet old lady and Rose appreciated the attention she was receiving from her.

"We influence what happens in the spirit world just as much as the spirits influence what happens to us, the living. There is a connection between this life and the hereafter...a wall that separates us but which may be breached."

"You're talking about Spiritualism, séances and Ouija boards and the like. I didn't know you believed in that stuff," Rose said.

"The spirit world is real, dear heart. It exists as a series of concentric spheres, emanating out from the center where God resides. There are seven layers all together. The inner six are occupied by spirits, striving to move from layer to layer toward the center. The outer layer is our world, the world of the living. When we die we enter the next layer. That is the one with which we can communicate."

"Hokus pokus. Weren't all those spirit mediums proven to be fakes?"

"Oh there were some that took advantage of the bereaved, fleeced them of their hard-earned dollars. But there were...there *are* many that are legitimate and sincere. They help others get through their grief. Once you've experienced communicating with a loved one who has passed, you no longer fear death for you come to realize that it is not an end, it's a beginning."

"But how do you know? Why do you, yourself believe?"

Elliot Cranston, who had been reclining in his favorite over-stuffed chair at the other end of the room began to cough loudly. His disruption of his wife's dialogue was not accidental. It was a signal to Mildred that his displeasure at her discourse on the supernatural was acute. He went so far as to toss a pillow across the room, knocking a stack of magazines off an end table.

"Ha!" he exclaimed. "Must be the spirit world trying to communicate with us." Mildred scowled, but discontinued her repartee.

Rose met her friend, Sara Ann, at Foster's Snack Shop after class. She had known Sara Ann since they were children growing up in Solon Springs and they had been best friends for most of that time. Sara Ann had been the one who had given Rose a ride in her car to the funeral. Sara Ann had cried during the service, having known Rose's family nearly all her life. Rose hadn't cried until later.

They sat in one of the wooden booths that lined the walls inside the snack shop, sipped coffee loaded with cream and sugar, and smoked filter-tipped cigarettes. A haze of smoke filled the booth and spilled out into the rest of the room. Rose told Sara Ann about her hallucinatory experiences—the tornado ceiling, the snake floor, the levitation and the ghostly hand. Sara Ann listened respectfully, without scorn or disbelief.

"Then Mrs. Cranston was talking about Spiritualism, like it was a religion. The spirit world overlaps our own at certain times," Rose said.

"I think maybe during your out-of-body experience you may have started to cross into the spirit world," Sara Ann offered. "You got their attention. One of them tried to contact you at the graveside."

"You think so? You think it was my father?"

"I don't know. Come back to the dorm with me. I want to show you something."

"College House? That spooky old building gives me the creeps. I don't know how you can stay there."

"Some people call it 'The Spook Temple.' Did you know it used to be the Morris Pratt Institute? The story goes that Pratt made his fortune after a spirit medium told him to invest in lumber and mining in Wisconsin. He built the huge house and gave lectures on psychic science and held séances. He started a school there in that building with a curriculum in Spiritualism."

"And you want me to come over so we can hold a séance? Really, Sara Ann."

College House was a stately three-story building in the Second Empire style with a mansard roof and an ornate double veranda. It featured two large plate glass windows topped by transoms decorated with stained glass in an abstract pattern. The roots of ancient ivy clung to the massive foundation stones and spidery traces of it were left on the bricks where caretakers had pulled the vines down. The girls entered at a smaller covered porch on the side of the building.

At the end of a long hall on the first floor was a lecture room with a stage and iron pillars supporting the upper floors. Upstairs on the second floor there were two more lecture rooms. On the third floor there were 12 dormitory rooms, but since the college had built a new girl's dormitory in 1950, few students had elected to room at the Spook Temple. Sara Ann had thought the old building quite elegant. She had heard the stories of ghosts and weird goings on that were associated with the former Morris Pratt Institute, but this intrigued her.

Later that evening Sara Ann had invited two of the other girls rooming at College House, named Ginger and Debra, to join them. The three of them had used a Ouija board to try contacting the spirit world many times, often with entertaining results. It was a popular parlor game—except that these young women sometimes took it seriously. An old Ouija board was placed on a table, the room was darkened, candles were lit, and incense of the pungent odor called patchouli was burned.

The Ouija was an old board of some uncertain wood, decorated at the corners with a grimacing sun face, a moon face crescent in profile, and various mysterious occult-looking designs. There were words on it written in a Gothic script: "yes," "no," "hello," and "goodbye." And in concentric arcs across the face of the stained and scared old board appeared letters of the alphabet and numbers.

Four pairs of hands touched lightly against the planchette, a small, three-legged table shaped like a heart and used as a pointer. The dead spirits soon would be talking through the medium of the Ouija board to the four live girls, or so it was hoped.

"Touch lightly with only two fingers," cautioned Ginger.

"Don't try either to move the planchette, or to hold it back. Just follow along with it," added Debra.

"What shall we ask it?" Sara Ann wanted to know.

"This is ridiculous," Rose felt compelled to say.

"Shh! You'll scare away the spirits if they think you're skeptical. Have an open mind, Rose. Shall we see if we can contact your ghost?"

"I don't have a ghost. I feel silly doing this."

"Quiet now!" The planchette began to move ever so slowly across the board.

"You're moving that!"

"No I'm not. There is a spirit present. Oh spirit, are you there?" Ginger chanted. The planchette moved toward the word yes and stopped, pointing to it.

"What is your name, spirit?" asked Sara Ann. The planchette began to move again, stopping to point at a series of letters. "A-F-I-H-O-W-Z," it had spelled out.

"Afihowz? What kind of a name it that?'

"It's a foolish one," said Rose. "This is clearly nonsense. I for one am bowing out. I have an early class tomorrow."

Snow was falling as Rose stood in the street looking up

at College House. On the mansard roof two dormitory windows showed light giving the place the appearance of a giant skull, dark against the night sky. One of the lighted orbs flickered—from candles, she knew, still in service to the three would-be mediums at play with their spook board. She was angry with herself for having expected—wished for some believable manifestation, a sound, a sensation, icy fingers clutching her shoulder—anything. Foolish girls! There are no ghosts.

Solon Springs sat on the west bank of a long, finger-shaped lake known as the Upper Saint Croix. The town's population numbered in the few hundreds and although it was a typical northern Wisconsin destination for fishing, hunting and boating, there were many year-round residents. The winter snows came early and stayed late into spring. Snow drifts three to four feet deep and temperatures well below zero were common. Winter could be brutal.

This one was an ordinary winter: snow was heaped onto the branches of fir trees, weighing them down; ice clung to the bare twigs of oaks and maples and caused them to glisten in the sun as if they were structures spun of glass; the tracks of rabbit, squirrel, raccoon, white-tailed deer and wolf broke up the smooth white snow cover which was unmarked by human footprints. The lake was frozen so solid that ice fishermen could drive their pickup trucks across its surface.

Rose was home for the holidays. It should have been a joyful time spent with family and friends, festive and filled with nostalgic memories of the ones now absent and missed. But depression had overcome her. Even the sparkling Italian lights her mother had strung on the Christmas tree couldn't cheer her. It wasn't that she missed her father: they hadn't been close these past few years—perhaps they'd never been close. No, it was something else, something she couldn't define. A feeling of dread that hung just outside of consciousness like an ache waiting to escalate into a pain.

It had something to do with her ghost—the one she insisted that she didn't have. There had been no recurrence of the psychic phenomena she had experienced previously.

No levitations or ghostly apparitions had come to plague her. Perhaps it was the *absence* of supernatural occurrences which troubled her. She knew something would come. She just didn't know when it would come or what it would be like. But she was certain that something was going to happen. Something unsuspected and unwelcome.

Christmas would be difficult with her father gone. Her mother had entered and exited each of the five stages of grief except the final one: acceptance. Her sister, Janet, was little help. Janet was six years younger than Rose, an accidental arrival in an inopportune chapter of their parents' lives: a livelihood stretched thin as rice paper at the loss of father's job; a remembrance all too vivid and disturbing of the recent loss of her older brother, Bryan, his fall from an adventurous climb up a water tower. And Rose, because her first days at school were her very first separation from family, felt she was being punished for something. She wasn't sure what.

Had Rose been asked to pen a narrative of her personal history, that year of Janet's birth, Bryan's death, et cetera, would have rated little attention. The effect those events had on her six-year-old self were now obscured by denial and selective memory loss. She simply didn't remember being present in the group of playmates who had congregated at the foot of the old wooden water tower urging Bryan to mount the rickety ladder, chiding him when he hesitated, cheering him on to the top, and running, screaming when he plunged to lie broken and bleeding before them.

Christmas dinner had been ordinary, except for the vacant space at the head of the table. Rose's Uncle Michael and Aunt Bertina and one of the cousins, Dotty, occupied one side of the table (the leaf having been inserted for the holiday meal), while Rose, Janet, and their other cousin, Robert, spread out along the other side. Rose's mother, June, sat at one end, staring across platters and bowls and candle sticks toward the empty chair where her husband would have sat and carved turkey and allocated drumsticks.

Uncle Michael worked at the coal docks at the twin ports of Duluth-Superior where the steel girders of giant cranes bristled out from the shores of Lake Superior like the spines of an enormous sea anemone. The towering structures extended out over thousand foot-long ore boats, unloading their cargoes of coal. Men like Uncle Michael rode in cabs along tracks on the great steel arms, dropping buckets suspended from cables down into the guts of the freighters. Jaws bit down on tons of coal which were lifted and carried back to be piled in mountains of gleaming ebony. Clouds of coal dust filled the air and covered the dock workers as thickly as if they had been down in the mines themselves.

Rose's father, Anthony, had worked along side of Uncle Michael until the day of the accident that had caused Anthony's termination from the docks. A bucket under Anthony's control had broken loose and plunged into the icy waters of Lake Superior taking its load of coal with it. Anthony had been blamed although the lack of maintenance of the crane was the probable cause. If you lived in Superior, Wisconsin, in the 1940s, you worked at the coal docks, the ore docks, or the railroad. If you had been fired from your job you had few options. Anthony, jobless and with a new baby in the household, was facing a bleak future when the news came that his wife June's mother had died.

After the death of their child and the loss of Anthony's job, this might have been the camel-back-breaking last straw except for the fact that an inheritance accompanied the bad news—not a staggeringly great one, but enough to grubstake a dream Anthony had harbored through all those years of grit and coal dust: his own roadhouse. Thus, along the shores of Upper Saint Croix Lake, near the highway down from Superior, at the hamlet of Solon Springs, the little restaurant and bar called the St. Croix Super Club was founded.

The super club did well, well enough to send Rose to college and start a fund for Janet. Anthony had achieved his dream and was happy beyond all reasonable expectations—and then he died. It was an almost embarrassingly normal death: a sudden collapse as he stood at the grill turning potato pancakes; a rush to the emergency room with wild sirens whining; a pointless defibrillator; the inevitable "I'm sorry to have to tell you..." from a serious, white-coated, young (June could only think of him as a kid) doctor—just your normal heart attack.

So there was an empty chair at Christmas dinner. Thankfully, thought Rose, Mother hadn't actually set a place for him! But his presence was felt in the small talk that skirted references to Anthony, the sly glances toward the empty chair, and the uncomfortable silence as Uncle Michael carved the turkey and allocated the drumsticks.

It was just before the pecan pie was served that the pounding started. Pounding and a clatter from above, as if someone had dumped a whole crane's bucket of coal onto the roof. It continued for several minutes while everyone sat paralyzed, unsure whether to duck or run. It trailed off into a dull rumble then suddenly ceased. Uncle Michael, Robert and Rose run to the front door, pulled it open and rushed out into the snow, craning their necks to examine the roof of the house.

A great deal of snow had been dislodged and the roof shingles showed evidence of damage, as if someone had been pounding on them with a hammer. As they kicked through the show drifts along the edge of the house they uncovered what appeared to be hundreds of fist-sized stones—stones that hadn't been there before.

"It must have been some of the neighborhood kids playing a trick on us. The little bastards," growled Uncle Michael.

"Poltergeists," said Robert. Rose suddenly felt faint and returned to the house.

Mildred Cranston, Rose's landlady, carried a tray of freshly baked snickerdoodles into the front room where Rose was curled into an over-stuffed chair. The old house was drafty and January temperatures assaulted it from every angle. Rose pulled a crocheted throw tightly around her shoulders and graciously accepted a warm cookie from Mildred.

"The Mister's snoring away in the study," said Mildred. "Elliot won't interrupt me this time while I tell you my ghost story."

"Why doesn't Mr. Cranston want you to talk about it?"

"Mr. Cranston is ashamed of my former life as a medium. Oh, don't think I was one of *those*, the ones that defrauded. I was just a girl, believing in what I *thought* was happening."

"Then you changed your mind?"

"Did you ever hear of the Wolf sisters? No? It was many years ago. Wolf is my maiden name. My sister Lucy and I...Lucy was two years older and I guess we were maybe eight and ten...we heard some knocking one night. That was strange because we were in our bedroom on the second floor and the sound almost seemed to come from right inside the room.

"We heard it again the next night, and the next, and although we tried to find the source of the sound we were quite stumped. We decided it was a ghost, trying to communicate with us for some reason. So we decided to ask it."

"Ask it? How could you do that?"

"We told the ghost to knock once for yes and twice for no and then we proceeded to inquire of it what it wanted. We first asked if it was a spirit. It knocked once for yes. 'Are you the spirit of someone who has passed over?' we asked. Again it answered with one knock for yes. We kept asking questions that could be answered with a yes or no and learned that it was a man who had once lived in our house but had died there. We then learned he had been murdered."

"Murdered! But how..."

"Someone had entered the house one night and murdered him as he slept. Well, you can imagine how we felt about that! We were terrified. But after that evening, the knocking stopped and we could learn no more."

"But you referred to yourself as a medium. Did you try to summon him again?"

"What happened was we told people what we had heard and learned. At first no one believed us. We insisted that it was all true and offered to demonstrate that we could 'talk to spirits' as we called it. We sat around a table in a darkened room, you know, the way they do, and held hands so we couldn't be doing the knocking ourselves. Well we never got our murdered man to come back, but we talked to some other spirits with our knocking technique and people began to believe us.

"Now the part of the story that makes Elliot ashamed is that some people wanted to exploit us. Charge people money to watch or participate in the séances. This of course attracted a great deal of attention and soon there were those who wanted to catch us cheating—show us up for frauds. And one evening a man who had come to the séance under false pretenses said he could tell that Lucy was causing the sounds. How? He didn't explain. But it was enough to put an end to our little enterprise. And for that I am glad. It was too frightening when I believed it and all too horrible to face the possibility that we were fakes."

"But didn't you know?"

"Not then. Later, Lucy confessed to me that she had learned how to crack her ankles in the dark to make the knocking sound. She said she just did it so that people would believe us. It just sort of got out of hand, I guess. But she insisted that the murdered man was a real ghost. She hadn't faked it that time."

"Unbelievable!"

"Yes, well the really frightening thing is that years later...we had moved out of the old house...someone was digging in the basement and they unearthed some old bones! We figured it was the body of the murdered man: our ghost."

Even by Midwestern standards the town of Wonewoc, Wisconsin was a tiny village. The highway through town followed the Baraboo River as it meandered beneath canopies of forest pine and raced past rocky crags above which turkey vultures endlessly circled, waiting to spy a dead river rat or chipmunk.

In the late nineteen century this serene, driftless area ("driftless" because the ancient glaciers that carved out Wisconsin's lakes had bypassed this region leaving the sculpting of the land to the rivers and the winds) attracted a group of Easterners searching for a peaceful setting in which to establish a retreat for followers of Spiritualism.

High on a bluff above the town they pitched their tents and then purchased an old school house in which they could hold meetings. The location would come to be called "Spook Hill" by the townspeople who were mistrustful of the strange goings on up there, the table rapping, the floating trumpets, the ectoplasmic materializations and other occult activities they imagined but could only speculate about.

But the spiritualist camp flourished and prospered, at least to the point that several dozen small cabins could be built, and by the 1950s the expanded camp grounds even had a bathroom and shower facility. It was shabby, but it was functional and during the summer season Wonewoc seemed to have as many "seekers" as it had residents— those hoping for contact with dearly departed family members, those wanting advice on whether to marry or buy a new car, those who had come to find and expose what they thought were fraudulent mediums, or those who simply wanted to rest and enjoy the beautiful surroundings.

Now Rose found herself once again crammed into Sara Ann's Volkswagen, this time puttering along highway 33. It was spring vacation and you were supposed to go to Fort Lauderdale or Daytona Beach, weren't you? But no, Sara Ann had insisted on an excursion to the Wisconsin Spiritualism Camp at Wonewoc. "You can relax there," she had said. "Maybe you'll find out something once and for all," she had said. "Maybe your ghost..."

"I told you, I don't have a ghost," complained Rose.

"So what was that apparition you told me you saw? The one at the foot of your bed? Just some bad pizza I suppose."

"I don't know. I...I wasn't feeling well. I couldn't sleep. Something...I thought I saw something. But probably it was just a shadow, or lights from a car coming through the window or..."

"Or bad pizza."

Rose hadn't told Sara Ann that there had been more than one appearance of the apparition. She had been awakened in the middle of the night by a loud thud and watched in disbelief as a faint light formed and grew into the proportions of a figure standing at the foot of her bed. Translucent in the dim light, it shimmered with a rhythm like the beating of her heart. The first time it appeared, it lingered only briefly and failed to resolve into a recognizable image before fading. On the second occurrence, the specter took on a human-like aspect, familiar, but still too vague to be identified as a person.

The third time was the charm: the figure had gained strength and apparent solidity—a man surrounded by a glowing aura stood motionless, his eyes reaching out to her from a face she had known all her life—her father's face, worn and worrisome and now, otherworldly. The spirit or specter or hallucination or whatever it was trembled slightly and its mouth moved soundlessly, as if it were attempting to vocalize some supernatural admonition. The effort must have robbed energy from the materialization process and so the figure dissolved into the darkness. Apparently returning to the world of the living wasn't easily achieved.

"You'd have thought this thing would have come with a radio," said Rose, referring to the car.

"Are you kidding? It doesn't even have a fuel gauge. When you run out of gas you switch over to the spare tank...oh, oh!"

"Oh, oh? I don't like the sound of 'oh, oh!' Don't tell me..."

"We're almost to Wonewoc. There will be a gas station there. At least I think there will."

They were lucky and rolled into the Sinclair station on Central Street just before the engine shuttered to a halt right in front of the pump. Perhaps Sara Ann had neglected to depress the clutch when she stepped on the brake peddle, or perhaps they were riding on the fumes from the empty tank, at any rate, the bright green pump with its familiar dinosaur logo (reminding eager consumers where fossil fuels came from) was a welcome sight.

A teenage boy in a stained tee-shirt wiped the windshield as gasoline glugged into the Beetle's tank. "Goin' up to Spook Hill?" he asked.

"Why would you get that idea," returned Sara Ann, a little annoyed at the boy's inquisitiveness.

"You sort of look like the type. Hope those witches don't take all your money." There was a small glass bubble on the face of the pump where you could see a little wheel spinning as gasoline pulsed through the bubble on its way to the hose. This was intended, Sara Ann supposed, to convince you that the pump was actually delivering product into your vehicle.

"That'll be two dollars and seventy-five cents," said the boy.

"Wise ass," grumbled Sara Ann as the VW spun back out onto the highway. She turned up Hill street and headed for the camp. Recent spring rains had turned the road into a set of muddy ruts, a bit wider than the Beetle's wheel base and the car slipped in and out of these, buffeting the girls. Miraculously, they made it to the camp without getting stuck in the mud. A series of weathered, white-washed cabins were arrayed along a circular path next to the road. These were set beneath tall pines that obscured the sun, creating a sort of perpetual twilight. They parked in front of a building with a hand-lettered sign reading "office."

"Jesus! It's like the Black Forest in here," said Rose.

Rose had had a sleepless night: she had elected to take the roll-away cot that had been provided to turn the small cabin into an abode for two, insisting that Sara Ann take the bed, although with the sagging mattress and creaking springs, Sara Ann might not have gotten the better bargain. There were no visitations by spirits or levitations that night, yet Rose did not feel at all relaxed. Her anxieties centered around her inevitable interaction with the camp medium, a plan put forth by Sara Ann which Rose would be expected to endure.

Yesterday they had been given a tour of the camp by a plump, squat, white-haired lady in an orange-flowered smock and open-toed shoes who reminded Rose a little of Mildred Cranston—in other words, another sweet old lady with a cleverly hidden dark side. Her name was Gladys Thornsbee and she was one of the two directors of the camp —the other director, a Mrs. Goodrich, was currently visiting relatives in Sheboygan. She gave readings, she said, and would conduct a séance tomorrow night if they were interested.

They had learned that the path where the cabins, a small chapel and a snack shop sat was called Harmony

Way, and that each cabin had a unique name descriptive of the miraculous experiences of former cabin dwellers. There was, for instance, one called Divine Content, and another called Spirit of the Pines. Their cabin was called Rainbow Enchantment, an appellation which conjured the anticipation of spectral visions and grand revelations for Sara Ann, but only brought a chuckle to Rose.

From Harmony Way a narrow path led through the woods to the top of a bluff called Meditation Point. Near the edge of the bluff sat a larger ramshackle structure, the old schoolhouse, now empty except for a circle of 13 chairs where, said their tour guide, the séance would be held.

Back at the office, Rose had looked at several framed pictures on the wall while Sara Ann registered. The paper label glued under the portrait of a gruff-looking man with a bald pate and full white beard identified the subject as Andrew Jackson Davis (1826-1910), the Poughkeepsie Seer, also known as the John the Baptist of Spiritualism. Another portrait, an austere looking woman in bonnet and shawl with a sharp nose that accentuated the sternness of her profile was labeled as Mother Ann Lee (1736-1784), the founder of the Shaker Movement.

After Sara Ann had registered them, Gladys Thornsbee had suggested readings as a sort of indoctrination (she called it an introduction) to spiritualism and a preparation for the séance, should they wish to participate in it. Sara Ann had agreed before Rose could object so now, this morning after a bad night's rest, they were headed up Harmony Way toward the little chapel where Gladys waited for them. Gladys brought them one at a time into a little room off the main meeting hall of the chapel. Sara Ann had her reading first, while Rose sat, attempting to meditate, but found her only thoughts were those that raised even more questions about the central issue: what in the world was she doing here?

When Rose's turn came the older woman, now dressed in a flowing white cotton robe and sandals, sat across from her at a small wooden table and took Rose's hands in her own. She began to talk softly about the people that came to the camp, what they sought, the help Gladys and others who plied their trade there had to offer. She did her best to put Rose at ease, and soon Rose was answering questions about her family and friends and—and this hadn't seemed inappropriate until she thought about it later—about Sara Ann.

The reading turned out to be an analysis of Rose's persona gleaned, it appeared to Rose, from the data Gladys had just collected and possibly from things Sara Ann must have told her. "Keep an open mind and avoid negative energy," Gladys told her. But she now felt even more estranged from the process of spiritual renewal that Gladys promised her. Rose really wanted to bolt but because Sara Ann was her best friend, a friend who had Rose's best interests at heart, she couldn't now abandon her. Besides, it was Sara Ann's car.

Later that afternoon Rose said to Sara Ann, "I don't want to go to that séance. It's too creepy. And ridiculous. I want to return home."

"Please go with me," Sara Ann said. "Do it for me. I've a feeling...something good is going to happen. For us both."

The circle had been drawn closer as not all thirteen chairs were filled. Candles flickered in the corners of the room and now six chairs held six seekers clasping hands and waiting for the séance to commence. Rose, torn between helping her friend (although why Sara Ann needed to be here escaped her) and wanting to run from the darkened chamber and away from these crepuscular, haunted woods, tried to summon as much negative energy as possible, thinking to derail the proceedings.

"Relax, Rose," said Gladys Turnsbee. "This isn't about you." She then closed her eyes and in a voice hardly above a whisper said, "Now we must all concentrate. Focus on the face of the loved one you wish to reach from across the veil."

There was dead silence coupled with an electric tension that moved from hand to hand, from person to person. Rose could feel it. Her breathing became short and quick. In the dim light, shadows seemed to move across her vision like black birds taking flight—it was only an effect of the candlelight, she reasoned.

"Mrs. Forester," said Gladys, breaking the silence, "your

husband is here again tonight. I can see him standing beside you." There was a gasp from Mrs. Forester, an elderly lady whose left hand held Rose's right, and which she squeezed so hard that Rose echoed her gasp.

"Yes...yes, I will tell her," continued Gladys. "He says that he is having a wonderful life in the beyond. He is happy and he is waiting for you to join him. He says it is a beautiful place and that you should not be afraid."

Mrs. Forester was sobbing quietly. "Oh, I'm so happy," she managed to say. Gladys now turned to the other side of the circle and spoke to a tall, middle-aged woman wearing what Rose thought was much too much jewelry which sparkled and glinted in the candle light.

"Mrs. Smiley...Agnes, I have asked the spirit guides to look for your son, Harold. But Harold has not crossed over yet. You will hear from the State Department soon. Yes, I know he was missing in action. And he nearly died. But the spirits feel it is not yet his time. You will see him again. Have faith."

"Are you sure?" asked Agnes Smiley. "It is torture not knowing for sure."

"I am sure, Agnes. My spirit guide is Wabokieshiek, also called White Cloud. He was a Winnebago medicine man during the Black Hawk wars in the nineteenth century. He has never let me down."

"An Indian!" exclaimed Rose, unable to contain her amusement. "How is it that he speaks such good English?"

"Rose, dear, all of those who go beyond can understand each other without language such as we know it. It is sort of like reading minds. Don't make fun of it, please."

"I'm sorry."

"Now I have to speak to Sara Ann. I am seeing a spirit standing beside you. It is hazy as yet. Now...now it is becoming more clear. Yes. It is a small child. A boy. He is here to tell you something, Sara Ann. What? His voice is so soft. He says...he says he doesn't blame you. He says it is all right. He is happy. You did nothing wrong. Does any of that make any sense to you?"

"What...what is his name? Do you know?"

"I'll ask, although he is beginning to fade. Spirit, what is your name? Ah. He says he is Bryan...Rose's brother,

Bryan."

"Bryan?" Rose called out. "What...why is Bryan appearing to Sara Ann? Bryan, my brother? Why would he blame..."

"Oh, Rose," said Sara Ann. "Don't you remember? When Bryan fell, I was one of those who had goaded him into climbing the tower. You were the only one who tried to stop him. I've always blamed myself for that."

"I tried to stop him? I don't...I don't remember anything about it. I did?"

"Yes you did. Now maybe both of us can have some peace of mind." There was a brief silence as the other seekers tried to comprehend what had just transpired. Revelations were always fascinating when they happened and they added positive energy to the séance. And they were entertaining.

Now Rose turned to Gladys Turnsbee, incredulous, but unsure of whether her mistrust of the spiritualist was based on logic or trepidation that all that had happened might just be true. "Is that all?" she asked. "Are there any more spirits present that you can see?"

"Why, no my dear. I see no other spirits."

"Oh? Not even *that* one?" Rose demanded, pointing to where she saw a shimmering form materializing from the gloom. But Gladys shook her head.

"Well, I see *my* ghost. He's right there in the center of the room. It's my father. Father...tell me...what do you want?" Gladys was dumbfounded. She saw nothing, no one. But this Rose was truly a psychic. Gladys had felt that from the first. If only the girl had been more open...

Rose repeated her question. The circle of seekers was stunned as they watched the girl rise up from her chair, dropping the hands of the other seekers. She almost seemed to float a few inches above the floor, but this must have been a trick of the light. Again she asked. "What? What...forgive? He said, 'Forgive!'" Then, suddenly, Rose collapsed into a heap on the floor.

Early the next morning the Volkswagen Beetle was zipping alone Highway 33 on the return trip to Solon Springs. The girls sat in silence, Rose, reluctant to talk and

Sara Ann afraid to broach the subjects of ghosts and the past. Their journey would take them east toward La Crosse and then up Highway 53 from the Mississippi River to Eau Claire and Chippewa Falls and a series of small towns, rivers and lakes. It was a four hour drive.

After about an hour Sara could contain herself no longer. "Rose, what did he mean, forgive? He couldn't mean he forgave you for causing Bryan's death, since you didn't, and being a spirit, he would know that."

Rose just stared out the window as they passed the pine forests, avoiding Sara Ann's eyes and her questions."

"Ah, maybe he wants you to forgive yourself. You've been blaming yourself, just like I did. That must be it. Well, now you can forgive..."

"Sara Ann! I don't want to talk about this!"

"I'm sorry. I was just trying to be a good friend. And I need to understand all this...supernatural stuff."

"He wants me to forgive *him*," Rose finally said.

"I don't understand."

"I never told you this...never told anybody. Not even Mother. But father..."

"What did he do to you, Rose? You can tell me. I wouldn't tell anybody. Did he..."

"When I was about ten he came into my room one night. He made me promise never to tell anyone. I was so ashamed! It went on for some time, then finally it stopped. I put it out of my mind. I was beginning to forget, to move away from it. Going to college helped a great deal. Well, then he died and it all came back to me, I guess."

"And now he is reaching out to you from beyond the grave. Asking you to forgive him."

"I still don't believe in that. I don't believe in his ghost. Don't you see? If he can really just be dead and gone then maybe I can begin to live my life as I should. But he haunts me! It's the worst thing I can imagine."

"Can you ever forgive him?"

"No. I can never forgive him, and he'll haunt me for the rest of my days."

They returned to the college at Whitewater. Rose moved from the Cranston's rooming house into the school's modern dormitory, explaining that she needed the society of other girls although it was really to distance herself from Mildred who had once been a medium. Rose and Sara Ann remained friends throughout their college years but never talked again about the camp at Wonewoc or what they had learned there. Rose continued to be haunted by...whatever it was.

In her senior year Rose met Jonathon Amberson, a handsome young man who was studying anthropology at the college. They began an affair and soon were slipping away to motel rooms or the rented apartments of friends where Rose experienced sexual gratification in a more or less normal manner—a gentle, loving interaction she had never imagined possible. After this, her father's ghost no longer came to stand at the foot of her bed.

A year after college graduation Sara Ann made the mistake of passing a slow-moving farm truck as it went around a blind curve. She was struck head-on by a vacationing couple driving a heavy station wagon and the VW crumpled up like a piece of discarded tin foil. She was killed instantly. Rose was devastated.

Rose stopped seeing Jonathon Amberson and retreated into a morbid state in which she rarely spoke to anyone. Her mother became concerned. Rose slowly recovered from grieving for Sara Ann but as she met and conversed with people she started to see apparitions again. This time they were not her own ghosts: they belonged to other people. She would tell the lady at the garden club or the postman or her uncle that a spirit was standing next to them and would receive responses ranging from laughter to scorn. It began to trouble her, almost as much as seeing her father's ghost once had.

Rose decided to return to the Wisconsin Spiritualist Camp at Wonewoc and talk to Gladys Turnsbee. She was a seeker again, this time seeking some kind of release from her visions. Gladys suggested that Rose was a natural medium, albeit a reluctant one. She offered her a position at the camp where she could explore her talent with the paranormal and in doing so help other people come to terms with their grief and their fears. Gladys was a very persuasive woman and Rose began sitting in on séances.

She could see the spirits but still could not talk to them. Gladys coached her, explaining the need to establish a rapport with the seeker in order to channel the spirit of the deceased. She soon became adept at interpreting the emotional situation unique to each seeker and to "read" a ghostly message to guide them appropriately. As she gained more experience working with seekers, she found one day that she now believed she could see and talk to the dead.

That was when Sara Ann appeared to her.

"Forgive me," Sara Ann implored Rose one night after materializing at the foot of her bed.

"I have nothing to forgive you for," replied Rose. "You must forgive me for not having believed in you."

"Do you remember how we played together as children?"

"Of course I do. It was a wonderful part of my life then...perhaps the only wonderful part."

"Did you know I sometimes came to your house when you weren't there? And your mother wasn't there? And your father..."

"Oh no, Sara Ann!"

"Forgive," said the spectre of Sara Ann as she faded away. It was the last time Rose ever saw her.

NOBODY LIKED LUDWIG

Nobody liked Ludwig. He had grown out of his cute puppy, big pawed, clumsy waddle, snuggle on your lap ways and developed a downright mean streak. He might snap at you or growl if you disturbed him in his sleep. He seemed incorrigible.

He was a classic short-haired dachshund, his smooth, cinnamon colored fur sleek and shining, his long torso and stubby legs initially laughable yet wonderful and curious in a way that made you wonder if God had somehow made a terrible mistake. His big brown eyes and floppy ears couldn't distract from a permanent snarl, upper lips revealing a menacing row of sharp, ivory colored teeth. Clearly, he was an unhappy critter. Nobody knew what had gone wrong. Nobody liked Ludwig.

Aunt Helen had wanted a doxie in the same way she had wanted Uncle Ed to buy a Buick instead of another one of those bland grey Plymouths he favored. Her bridge partner, Bernice, had one and bragged incessantly about her little Wolfgang's cute antics. It was a matter of prestige for Aunt Helen: a wiener dog was all the rage.

When the new pup was brought home and duly registered with the Kennel Club, he was cloistered in the kitchen on a freshly washed and folded bath robe that Uncle Ed, Helen was sure, would never miss. In the cutest little way he proceeded to rip it apart. Still, everyone thought Ludwig was the greatest thing since sliced bread.

But when shoes and the legs of furniture began

exhibiting the marks of tiny teeth and ominous wet spots appeared on the carpet, Ludwig's appeal began to ebb. Uncle Ed was given walk duty in an effort to allow the puppy to do his business outdoors. Ed appreciated the chance to puff on his briar pipe which Helen didn't allow him to do in the house, but was annoyed at the dog's constant pulling at the leash. Ludwig, himself annoyed at not being allowed to sniff and run after squirrels, learned how to hold his business until they returned to the house where upon he deposited said business and kicked it under the furniture to be discovered at a later time.

Ludwig never connected the harsh tirades hurled against him with any misbehavior on his own part since the act and the result were so removed in time. Luddie, for that was one of his other names, along with "Stupid Mutt" and "Damn Mongrel," could always tell when the humans addressed him by the acrid timbre of their maledictions. Sometimes in a condescending whine or the rumbling crescendo of threatening phrases he recognized the few words that he knew like "bad dog," or "God Damn it," but to him these were not associated with anything in his dog reality. More often than not, they preceded a swat on the nose with a rolled up newspaper. This particular action he interpreted as an invitation to the game of "grab it and run," which in turn precipitated more harsh reproaches.

Luddie's adopted family included my cousin, Annie, a skinny blond girl who didn't mix well when she and I and our other cousins got together on holidays or summer vacations. She was shy and withdrawn and, shall I say it?— sensitive.

Annie must have been about ten when Aunt Helen took her and Ludwig downtown to Harvey Pearson's Professional Photography Studio on Walworth Street to sit for a 14 by 17 sized hand-colored photograph. Aunt Helen wanted to rescue some prestige from the disaster of the insubordinate dog (and also needed to fill a large gold-leafed frame she had bought to hang above the piano).

Annie always reminded me of the fable of the princess and the pea, the one in which many mattresses are stacked on top of a single pea which the princess still can feel, being a delicate, sensitive type. Years later, in my Comparative Psychology Class at college, my professor pointed out the obvious sexual symbolism in that story. Be that as it may, to me, Annie was just a delicate, sensitive type, prone to bursting into tears at inexplicable instances for reasons unfathomable to the rest of us.

You could see it in the photograph. If you looked closely, you could tell the retoucher had struggled to hide the trails of tears on Annie's checks, the slight redness around her eyes. And yet, the tightly braided pig tails falling nearly to her waist, the gentle, if forced, curve of her lips as she affected a smile, the little dog sprawled across her lap, together created a romantic scene of a girl and her dog. For Aunt Helen, it was a Renoir and an emblem of the life she thought she ought to have. But looking closely at the dog in the picture you could sense a flicker of murder in his eyes and a slight pulling up of the upper lip, perhaps in anticipation of the clamping of those jaws down on the arm of Harvey Pearson, Professional Photographer.

The ultimate humiliation and insult came when Uncle Ed purchased the choke collar. This was a silver chain that looped through itself, allowing the dog walker to close it tightly around the dog's neck. The more the dog pulled against it, the tighter it got. When Uncle Ed stopped to dip a flaming farmer's match into the bowl of his pipe, he could give a quick flick of the leash and Ludwig would be immobilized and demoralized with a single jerk. I always thought the choke collar was what had put Ludwig over the edge.

One blue blustery day in March with the remnants of winter still wafting in the wind, Ludwig decided to take it on the lam. No one had hooked the front screen door and a swift push of the nose facilitated Luddie's escape. He stopped briefly, turned back toward the dysfunctional family dwelling he had called home during his formative years, gave a weak yip and trundled down the walk.

At the front gate, conveniently left open, he paused again, brushing against the fence post like a cat marking its territory. He might have thought, "Call me a stupid mutt, huh? We'll see about that!" With a deft twist of his head he had looped the dreaded choke collar around a stake holding up the post and slipped elegantly out of it. He was gone.

The next day, Saturday, I had gone to my Aunt's house to borrow a skein of yarn for my mother. Annie was in the living room, crying. I didn't think much about this at first but something about the intensity of her sobs gave me pause.

"What's wrong?" I asked.

"Ludwig is gone," came the answer. "He ran away."

"But," I insisted, "you all hated that dog!"

A frosty stare confronted me and I didn't pursue that line of reasoning any more. I gave a glance up at the portrait of Annie and Ludwig hanging over the piano. Something intermingling love and hate, sadness and desire seemed to emanate from it. Just at that moment, Aunt Helen entered the room, trailing with her the scent of air freshener and furniture polish. She acknowledged me with a nod, then focused on Annie, whose checks were still damp from tears.

"Stop sniveling," she retorted. "Act your age, girl!"

It was then that I knew why Annie had been crying. It was not for the loss of the dog. It was because Ludwig had escaped—she could not.

*   *   *

A light drizzle is falling against the rough surface of the bridge, forming tiny rivulets that meander to the edge and drop like a beaded curtain to the dried up creek bed below. Underneath the bridge stands a boxy structure of odd angles and mismatched materials: some wood, some rusty metal, some stained and wrinkled cardboard. Across one side, upside down, is lettering that reads "Amana," and some Chinese characters. On another side is hung a coarse and ragged blanket, its color no longer distinguishable from the dirt and grime that clings to it. Outside of this dubious edifice is a single flower pot containing a single bloom that might have looked real had it not been a bright phosphorescent blue.

A small brown creature approaches, seeking shelter from the rain. Above, in the fragile branches of a Ginko tree, a morning dove hoots a plaintive warning. Young squirrels scatter, still testing their ability to bounce away from danger.

The interloper pauses when he sees the box, the scent of humans awaking old trepidations. But hunger overcomes fear and he noses aside the blanket, probing the interior with a caution recently learned. He hears a duet of snorts and snores and recognizes this sound as safe passage for his foraging: the humans are asleep. Right away he locates a paper bag containing some stale slices of bread and gobbles these hurriedly, chewing down some of the paper as well. He feels a large hand pressing his back and turns, prepared to snap.

"Whoa there, buddy boy! I ain't gonna hurt ya!"

There are no familiar words in this human's utterance, no tonality that he can reference as ridicule or rebuff. The hand strokes him gently, momentarily calming him, raising his curiosity, staying his defensiveness.

"Now then, little fella. You hungry?" And turning to his companion, the man says, "Look, Sal, a little doggie."

"Oh, how cute," says Sally. "It's one of them wiener dogs."

She rummages through a pile of old clothing and comes up with another paper bag, this one containing the remnants of a chicken leg. She holds it out to the dog who snaps it out of her hand nearly taking off a finger.

"He's a hungry little tike, ain't he?"

The hungry little tike is bedraggled, spattered with mud, dotted with burrs. He has a deep scar across his snout, the result of a dispute with another feral canine over a discarded pork chop. His once portly physique now exhibits ribs and shoulder bones giving him a sharpened contour. He has endured several harrowing weeks of his elected independence from humankind and through the hard knocks of arduous subsistence, learned to survive. It hasn't been an easy education. Now he is confronted with a dilemma: to surrender to the enemy in return for succor, or to flee, once again out into the cruelty of the wild and brutal world.

"Joe, he's got no collar," says Sally. "Let's keep him."

"One more mouth to feed," complains Joe. But looking into that pair of deep brown eyes he sees desperation and feels a kindred linkage to misery existing between him and the dog. "Of course we'll keep him, if he'll stay, that is."

"What should we name him?

"How about 'Dog'?"

"We'll name him Little Oscar, after Oscar Meyer."

"You're always thinking about food, old girl."

Joe always calls Sally "old girl" even though she is younger than he and he is only twenty. Twenty, but he feels more like sixty, what with the aches and pains, the sleeping on cold hard dirt, the eating out of trash cans when they can't panhandle enough money for food. What he would really like is to go to Florida. If they had the money...

"And speaking of food..."

The rain has stopped. Joe throws off the blanket. They are both fully dressed for there is no purpose to getting undressed, just to sleep in the cold. Joe considers finding some rope to tie to Oscar, but thinks better of it. The dog will follow, or he won't, he reasons. Sally pulls some of the burrs from the dog's fur and tries brushing off the mud with the back of her hand. Uncharacteristically, Oscar allows this. He has surrendered.

There is a chop suey joint on the south side of town where they can set up for panhandling and hit the cans in the alley behind if they have no luck. Sally squats down against the building and holds a sign reading "Down on our luck." Joe stands, partially blocking the sidewalk, his hand held outward, an injured look in his eyes. Oscar nuzzles up to Sally and she hopes he will illicit sympathy from passersby.

"Did I ever tell you about my cousin, Jerry, who played Little Oscar?" asks Joe.

"What, you have a cousin who's a midget?"

"No, a Little Person. He wasn't the famous one, the one from the Wizard of Oz movie. But he drove around in that wiener car when they took it to Cleveland."

"Joe, you never cease to surprise me.

"Having a midget cousin?"

"No, living in Cleveland! You never told me you lived in Cleveland."

"I was born there."

"Told me you was from Chicago, Joe."

"I ran away to there. As a teen."

"Your Pa beat on you like mine did me?"

"My Pa left when I was 5."

"Yer Ma then?"

"She drank. Took in men. I left. Like my Pa.

It is early in the day, and no one has come up the sidewalk. Dark clouds are forming, threatening a return of the cold rain and bitter wind that will drive them back into their sanctum under the bridge. Joe thinks about his childhood then throws away the thoughts as he has learned to do over time. He thinks about when he first met Sally, another teenager, the two of them living off the street, hanging around the vegetable market, waiting for the odd crate of produce to tumble from a truck or scrounging in the ash cans for anything useful. Why'd I ever hook up with you old girl, he asks himself. Out loud he answers, "Somebody had to take care of you."

"Oh, Joe!" Sally squeezes the little dog against her chest. Oscar, who used to be known as Ludwig, squirms free, then settles back down on her lap, glad for the attention, glad that these two humans talk to each other with soft voices, not like the badgering and bickering of his former humans.

"Somebody coming!"

The man is tall but lanky. His trench coat is unbuttoned and flaps about in the brisk breeze that has begun to blow papers and scraps of debris along the street. He sees Joe straddling the sidewalk before him and tenses. Joe's hand is stretched out toward him.

"Can you help us, mister?" Joe ask

"Go away," the man growls. "You'd just spend it on drink, ya bums!"

Joe is shaken by the accusation. He has never touched liquor himself, having watched what it had done to his mother. He wants this man to understand that, but he is unable to speak, and just stands his ground, his arms dropping to his sides. The man suddenly pushes at Joe, the impact toppling Joe to the sidewalk. Oscar has been growing anxious through all this and has wound up tightly like a steel spring. He leaps at the man, his teeth finding the flesh of the man's leg. A thousand years of ancestry to the wolf emerges in Oscar's small breast. He rends and tears at the man's limb as if he is bringing down a great stag for the pack. The man screams, kicks the small dog loose and runs. Sally manages to grab and hold Oscar before he can give chase. Joe picks himself up. It has all happened so fast he is stunned, unsure for a moment even of where he is.

The first heavy drops of rain are falling, hitting the pavement with explosive little bursts. Oscar has found something on the sidewalk and is clenching it in his teeth, shaking his head and growling angrily. Sally stoops down and tries to retrieve what ever it is from the dog but he hangs on with determination and that special strength of will that small dogs possess in great quantity. She can see now what it is: the man's wallet.

*   *   *

Oscar slept in the cardboard shack every night, waiting for his adopted family to return. Joe and Sally had taken the money from the wallet and bought bus tickets to Florida, leaving the small dog to fend for himself. Oscar didn't understand why they had gone, or where, but kept faithful vigil under the bridge. He found food in the cans in the alley behind the chop suey joint and stealthily avoided all contact with humans.

One night he heard a loud rumbling and left the shack to investigate. A hard rain had fallen for days and the trickle of water in the creek bed had become a substantial torrent. As he looked up stream he was horrified to observe a wall of water rushing down at him with the furry of a locomotive at full throttle. A dirt dam built to divert creek water into a lagoon had been washed away in the storm and the lagoon was emptying its contents in a massive deluge into the meager waterway. Oscar scampered up the bank in time to witness his shack being carried away, tumbling and breaking up in the swift current. Where once had been the potential of a happy home, there now was only a swirling maelstrom of muddy water.

He found a discarded cardboard box in the alley behind the chop suey joint and slept there, the smell of rancid rice and spoiled pork dampening his desire for food, but not quelling his hunger. Would Joe and Sally set up panhandling shop again outside the restaurant and find him once again? Or would the evil man who had pushed Joe come along and disrupt his new found equanimity? The scraping of tiny feet told him he was not alone in the alley. A family of long-tailed rats were also perusing the trash receptacles. He barked to frighten them away, a useless gesture, and one that, perhaps, led to his next adventure.

For as he stood on his stubby hind legs, front paws and nose working open the lid to a garbage can, he was enshrouded in the coarse mesh of a net. With the sound of heavy footfalls and a "Got 'em!" he was swiftly lifted and ungraciously tossed into a dark place, a place that roared and shook and began to move. After a while he was again lifted and tossed, this time freed of the net but enclosed in cubicle with walls and ceiling of metal fencing. There was room to turn around—just barely. And turn round he did. And round and round and round, barking his high pitched bark until he had exhausted himself.

For a long time he was alone although he could hear other dogs barking and clawing at their own cages. A dish with water and another with some dried food were brought and he tried to escape when the door opened, but strong hands held him down and other hands circled his neck with a collar. It was the first time he had worn a collar since the old days, days that seemed so long ago, so dimly remembered and unhappy in that remembrance.

Days passed and he grew used to a certain routine. He had been bathed. He had food, water and was taken out to an exercise yard once a day where he could run and nip at other dogs. He became passive, more calm and even respectful of his jailers as they treated him well, even talked to him in lowered voices. From time to time other humans would walk by the cages and some would look at him and comment, but he didn't know any of the words that were used, nor did he recognize inflections in the voices. At least he was dry and more or less warm. But not free.

He eventually got to know the other dogs, at least in the manner that dogs can know one another. In the exercise yard they became a temporary pack, with hierarchies established and maintained by the dogs alone.

Occasionally, one of the other dogs disappeared and he never saw them again. New dogs would join the pack and would be initiated into the hierarchy by the more important dogs. It was something they understood instinctively and accepted as part of the natural order of things. There was a female terrier that he particularly liked, but one day she too was gone.

There were several jailers he had gotten to know. One day two of them, a man with a gruff voice and a woman with a musical tone to hers stood outside his cage talking. He sensed an emotional lilt in their voices that saddened him although he couldn't understand their words. That they were discussing him, of that he was sure. He recognized the phrase, "the poor little fellow." The woman retrieved a ribbon from where it was tied in her hair and unlatched the cage door.

"Here, this will make him stand out. Seem more special." And with that she tied the ribbon into a bow around his collar. "One more day," she said. "One more day and the thirty day waiting period is over."

"I know," said the man.

"I hate seeing these animals destroyed just because nobody wants them."

"I know," said the man, shaking his head. "I know."

On the following morning, the sun shone brightly through the window, casting crazy shadows of the metal cage onto the floor. Oscar lazily lapped water from his bowl, eager to join the other dogs in the exercise yard. Two pairs of shoes entered his field a view, one small pair and one larger pair. He looked up and saw a young boy clutching the hand of a tall woman.

"Gramma!" said the boy. "This one is so cute. Can I have this one, Gramma?"

"Are you sure you don't want the other one, Peter?" asked the woman.

"No. This one! Look, he has a bow!"

"Will you promise to walk him every day and feed him and give him water?"

"Oh, I will! I will! I promise, Gramma. Can we take him home?"

Later that day, Oscar, formerly known as Ludwig and

soon to be called by yet another name, went to live with Peter and his grandmother at her apartment in the city. The grandmother, a widow, had taken the boy to live with her after his parents were killed in an automobile accident a few years before. The boy needed something young and active in his life she knew, and the idea of a dog came to her mind. A small dog that could be managed in the apartment, one that would give Peter a sense of responsibility as well as an enjoyable diversion—that was just what the doctor ordered.

The Elderberry Apartments overlooked the park, just across the street. Peter could walk the dog there without his grandmother having to worry about him. Peter, Gramma, and Oscar arrived there by taxi and took the elevator to the fourth floor, avoiding the questioning looks of Walter, the doorman. Once in the apartment, Oscar was in a daze. There were soft looking chairs and a sofa, a comfortable appearing rug, windows to look out of—a wonderful variety of places for napping! To his surprise, the boy gave him a hug. The woman led him into the kitchen where she poured some water into a bowl and placed it on the floor.

"Welcome," she said, "to your new home."

THE BALLOON ASCENSIONIST'S WIFE

Had they been born and raised in the same small Wisconsin town the boy and the girl would surely have become childhood companions. On dusty back roads, kicking the round green missiles of the fallen walnuts at invisible targets, they would have shouted in glee. In gardens dripping wisteria from rotting trellises, staring into the gazing globe with eager eyes, they would have laughed at the pinched faces, anamorphic and askew, that stared back. Along walks of brick or cobble, racing with sticks dragged against pickets creating clattering commotion, they would have awakened dogs in yards, adding barking to the bedlam. Behind barns in the protective thickness of bushes, they would have explored their differences.

He roamed trash-filled, rain-wet alleyways: a city boy, perhaps kicking cans. She strolled country lanes and village sidewalks, fall-carpeted with deep reds and copper oranges and the faded yellows of maple, elm and oak: a country girl, perhaps skipping rope. They would meet—but not yet.

The boy, his name was Peter Cummins, was all of fifteen years old in the spring of 1856 when the Haggenbach and Willis Circus with its tents splendidly white against the azure sky set up just a few miles outside of Milwaukee. Growing up in Wisconsin, Peter was not unfamiliar with circuses, but this one featured an act that captured Peter's imagination: the Flying Levitt Brothers, a trapeze act in which one of the brothers executed a triple somersault.

Thrilled spectators gasped in unison as Simon Levitt in sequined tights, leaped into empty air, tucked and tumbled once, twice, three times, and hung momentarily suspended against the darkness of the canvas ceiling, then swooped toward the sawdust thirty feet below and connected, hand against arm and arm against hand, with his brother aerialist at the last possible second. Peter Cummins marveled at this spectacular feat and it was then that he knew the future he wanted to follow.

Peter attended all three days that the circus stopped over at Milwaukee, drinking in the ambient pageantry and the intoxicating energy of the circus performers. He studied the aerialists and saw how essential timing was to their stunts. By the last day he felt brave enough to venture through the canvas flaps that hid the inner workings of the circus from the crowd. He passed a line of equestrians waiting for their entrance, bumped elbows with strangely costumed clowns and acrobats, slipped along the sides of cages smelling of monkey or tiger, and found the dressing area used by the Flying Levitt brothers.

The girl, her name was Cassandra Bentley, was only thirteen years old in the fall of 1856 when the Haggenbach and Willis Circus returned to its winter quarters in Delavan, Wisconsin. Cassie's parents had moved from their farm into town six years before. Mr. George Bentley, Cassie's father, had gone into partnership with a man named Hollingsworth and had opened a livery and harness maker's establishment on Walworth Avenue; this move occurred on the heels of the arrival of the first of the many circuses which would winter in this small Southeastern Wisconsin town.

George Bentley was careful to counsel his only daughter about the evils of circus people: their low-life mannerisms, their fondness for drink, their loose morals. When he had come to Delavan he had witnessed a piousness instilled in the populace, the result of the town's founding fathers' faith in teetotalism. No wonder—as the town and the county had been named for those staunch men, leaders in the Temperance League, E. C. Delavan and C. R. Walworth respectively. Now things were changing. Saloons had sprung up like weeds. Exotic animals were led through the streets by their handlers. Ragged men, roustabouts, were to be seen everywhere. Delavan was getting a reputation as a "wild little city." The circus had come to town.

Cassie was wary of the rough-looking circus men who came to her father's harness shop to purchase tack for their horses. There were often unusual requests: harnesses and saddles made to fit camels; trick-riding saddles equipped with special handles made of soft, quilted padding; braided bullwhips with long horsehair crackers; a tiger-sized saddle with monkey-sized hand grips. One day, Simon Levitt and a young boy came into the shop when Cassie was helping her father. The young boy looked especially seedy to Cassie.

"I have an strange request," Simon Levitt told George Bentley. "I want you to construct a special halter to fit this boy here."

"What kind of halter would that be?" inquired Bentley.

"I've embarked upon an attempt to train this lad in the art of trapeze acrobatics. We work close to the ground but he keeps falling. I want a halter we can hook to a wire. When he loses his grip on the bar we'll float him over the crowd. It'll be a great effect!"

George Bentley considered this. All these circus people were crazy, he believed—this just confirmed that fact. However, the challenge to make a halter to support the boy's weight intrigued him. "All right," he said. "Have the boy stand here for measuring. Cassie, get the tape."

As Bentley wrapped the cloth tape measure around the boy's waist Cassie wrote the numbers on a pad of paper. She caught a look of embarrassment on the boy's face. She smiled.

"Child! What do you find so funny?" the boy demanded.

"Child? I'm not a child! You...you...bumpkin!"

So went the first unfortunate meeting of Cassie Bentley and Peter Cummins. The very next year, Cassie saw an early season performance of the Haggenbach-Willis Circus as they prepared to leave Delavan for the summer tour. During the trapeze act, a clown dressed in baggy pants and huge shoes climbed a rope ladder to the small platform where the Levitt Brothers were executing aerial stunts, swinging from trapeze bars by their knees, doing flips and somersaults and generally amazing the crowd. From that precarious height the clown grabbed a trapeze bar and swung out into midair over the circus ring. The crowd roared with laughter at his clumsy antics—then suddenly he slipped from the bar. The wire attached to Peter Cummins' halter supported him as he flapped his arms like a gigantic and ungainly bird and was maneuvered out over the heads of the audience. Peter had finally become a flier.

In the autumn of 1859 the Walworth County Fair was drawing scores of visitors to the fairgrounds in Elkhorn where the main attraction was a new pastry treat called a cream puff. Professor Miraculous, his real name was Seymour Walsh, had a hot air balloon tethered on the midway. For a dime a fair patron could climb wooden stairs and enter the basket suspended beneath the balloon. Professor Miraculous then released one set of tethering lines to allow the balloon to rise to the dizzying height of thirty-five feet at which time another strong rope attached to a stake on the ground prevented the balloon from drifting away.

A spectacular view of the fair was thus achieved by anyone who dared to make the ascension. For added safety, the Professor's young assistant accompanied the balloon passengers in the basket and pointed out various landmarks until the balloon was pulled back to earth by a hand-turned winch. Professor Miraculous' Balloon Ascension became one of the most popular rides at the fair, second only to the "Ship of the Desert," an aged camel on loan from one of the circuses.

Cassie Bentley was now a very sweet sixteen with light brown tresses and a blossoming figure that turned many young heads, much to the dismay of her father. She had been allowed to attend the fair under the supervision of her Aunt Llewellyn, her father's sister, a stiff-backed matron with a dour disposition. Cassie pulled her aunt rapidly from booth to booth, purposely trying to tire the woman. But Aunt Llewellyn was undaunted in her devotion to the stewardship of her niece and kept pace admirably. When Cassie saw the multicolored banner announcing Professor Miraculous' Balloon Ascension she thought she had found a good opportunity to escape from her aunt, if only for a few moments.

"Come on, Auntie Lu," she said. "Let's go up in the balloon!"

After some awkward negotiations Auntie Lu relented to letting Cassie go up in the balloon while she, Llewellyn, stayed on terra firma in a state of anxiety bordering on panic. It happened that Cassie was the only passenger for this ascension. As the young assistant helped her into the basket, Cassie might have recognized Peter Cummins, the smart aleck circus boy of several years ago, but she did not. Peter also failed to notice anything familiar about the brown-haired lass yet his interest was aroused by her slender form and the enchanting arch of her body as she stood on tiptoes to peer over the rising basket's edge.

"What's your name?" he asked.

"Cassie," she replied, but did not inquire as to his. Perhaps she was distracted by the inspiring vista of the fairgrounds below. The wind against her face and hair had a chill that she hadn't expected: it was exhilarating. At the end of the restraining rope the balloon swayed and turned slowly. She could see out over the Wisconsin landscape, the fields, the farmhouses, the roads and rivers—a miniature map of her world, laid out in a patchwork quilt of autumn color. She had no fear of the height; she was in awe of this new view of the universe.

"Are you enjoying this?" Peter asked her. She nodded. "Would you like to go flying?" he asked. Again she nodded, perhaps taking his suggestion as a frivolous query instead of the serious proposal that it was.

"I'm Peter, by the way," he added as he slipped the loop of the tether off of its peg. It took some seconds before Cassie realized that the balloon was drifting away from the fair.

Cassie would remember that wild ride (and especially the wrath of her aunt and her father) for years to come. Their combined fury at her recklessness overwhelmed her and perhaps dampened her desire for adventure, at least for several months after the incident. Peter too, upon his return to the fair, had been accosted by an irate Professor Miraculous: the boy's position was immediately terminated. In spite of these setbacks, the boy and the girl thought back on their flight fondly as a wondrous expedition into high adventure.

Pushed by wind—earth's very breath—the balloon, buoyant with heated air from the charcoal fire back at the fairgrounds, had maintained altitude long enough to carry them over treetops and church steeples, over flag poles and telegraph poles, and across fields where farmers toiled cutting corn and wheat. They were wafted over low rolling hills where summer green merged with the browns and ochers of autumn; toward kettle-like depressions in the landscape dug by ancient glaciers, home to badgers and porcupine; to a shimmering dash of aquamarine that dominated the terrain beneath them as the slowly cooling air in the balloon lost lifting power over Lake Beulah.

Wind. A gentle kiss of wind had rocked the basket like a cradle. A puff, a gust, a tiny turbulence had spun the bulbous ball of oiled fabric above them like some god-like child playing with a toy. A sudden zephyr of a tailwind had caught them and pushed them along barely a few feet above the surface of the lake. As the basket dipped lower and lower and began to skip and skim Lake Beulah's choppy water, Peter wrapped his arms around Cassie and asked, "Can you swim?"

"Of course I can swim, silly." Cassie answered.

Peter plunged into the cold water carrying the girl with him. The basket scooped into the lake bringing the balloon's frantic dash to an abrupt halt. The balloon collapsed on top of the basket and the entire soggy mess began to sink. Peter had gotten them clear of the crashing balloon just in time, probably saving their lives. Cold and wet, the boy and the girl had dragged themselves out of Lake Beulah and wandered aimlessly for hours until they found a farm house and a sympathetic farmer's wife.

The incident was not without its repercussions. Weeks later, Peter Cummins tried to see Cassie at her house but

Cassie's father met him at the door. Circus riffraff were not allowed into the Bentley household, he was told. Endangering the girl like that was unforgivable, George Bentley told Peter. The sheriff might be interested to learn that a vagabond rascal such as he was lurking about town. Discouraged, Peter left Delavan the next day to meet up with a circus that was traveling through Ohio and Indiana.

A young man named William Wilkinson had better luck in his approach to Cassie Bentley. His father was president of one of Delavan's leading banking establishments, a fact that helped to soften George Bentley's restrictions on his daughter's love life. Cassie had known Willie in school, but their paths had seldom crossed as children. George Bentley approved of Wilkinson, or at least, of his family's prominence in the town. Willie and Cassie stepped out together in the following months.

Cassie liked the shy young man with his polite manners and his knowledge of literature and poetry. His nose, she felt, was a bit hawk-like, but this gave him an appearance of sincerity: the countenance of a charming man-about-town was impossible for him to mime. They spent long hours sitting on the hill above the creek on a flagstone wall, watching swallows flitting through the willows, talking of Blake and Wordsworth.

Leaves in muted fall colors now lying on the ground were lifted and spun by miniature whirlwinds, crisp little breezes foretelling winter's chill. Nothing other than nature's pageantry affected the young couple, certainly not politics. In October, when John Brown attacked the armory at Harper's Ferry in Virginia, they were oblivious to its implications. During the next year when political turbulence tugged at the Union's very fragile foundations, Willie and Cassie were contemplating the formation of their own union.

Cassie's father insisted she wait at least until she was eighteen to marry the lad—another whole year! Willie suggested elopement, a brash proposal quite out of character for the mild-mannered young man. Cassie was sensible for once and followed orders, telling Willie she was unready for the transformation into wife and mother. Willie was abashed, demoralized; his impatience funneling umbrage into anger. There was a spat, a lovers' quarrel, a split—then surely as blushing spring banished frigid winter, there was reconciliation, reaffirmation, and renewal. Springtime also brought an attack on Fort Sumter, its surrender to Confederate General P. G. T. Beauregard, a declaration of insurrection by President Abraham Lincoln and a call for volunteers. Willie Wilkinson volunteered.

The scene at the train station in Madison, Wisconsin, on June 11, 1861, was a poignant one as the Second Wisconsin Volunteer Infantry Regiment, mustered in by Colonel S. Park Coon, prepared to embark for Washington, D. C. where they would come under the command of William Tecumseh Sherman. One month later they would engage in their first combat at the Battle of Bull Run. The regiment would become part of the Iron Brigade of the Army of the Potomac and fight throughout the war until the Battle of Gettysburg, the turning point of the American Civil War. A tearful Cassie Bentley waved a wrinkled handkerchief as the train steamed away.

* * *

A man named Professor Thaddeus Sobieski Constantine Lowe, a showman and balloonist, intended to make the very first transatlantic balloon flight. In April of 1861, shortly after the attack on Fort Sumter, the professor embarked from Cincinnati on a test flight of his new balloon. Nine hours later, the westerlies had blown him over South Carolina, the first state to have seceded from the Union. Lowe's balloon descended in the town of Unionville. The local residents, after examining the sack of abolitionist literature he had, for some unknown reason, brought along with him, decided he was a Union spy and detained him. They threatened him with imprisonment.

Fortunately for T. S. C. Lowe, a local businessman, the proprietor of a hotel, knew Lowe and vouched for him. He was released. (He would later make claim to having been the first Northern prisoner of war.) Something about the experience gave him the idea to suggest the use of balloons for warfare. By July he had demonstrated balloon ascension for Abraham Lincoln, telegraphing the President from his balloon, the Intrepid. After competing with three other prominent balloonists, Lowe was contracted to observe enemy troop movements and soon found himself at the Battle of Bull Run.

Lowe's balloon floated behind enemy lines. Before Confederate soldiers discovered him he was found by the 31st New York Volunteers. His rescue, however, could not be accomplished by the Union soldiers as Lowe had twisted his ankle badly upon landing and could not walk. His wife, Leontine, disguised herself as an old woman and traveled safely in a buckboard, hid Lowe under a tarp and brought him back to Ohio.

The significance of this near disaster had two results: Lowe realized that the balloon would have to be stationary, not floating, to make observation of the enemy practical; and a few of the generals saw the potential of the balloon in warfare. Lowe was allowed to create the Union Army Balloon Corps. It consisted of seven hydrogen-filled balloons and operators drawn from civilian amateur and professional balloonists.

A handful of enlisted men were assigned to the Balloon Corps. They worn an insignia on their caps: a metad in the shape of a balloon with the letters, "BC" emblazoned on it. One of these men was on loan from the Army of the Potomac's Iron Brigade—Private William Wilkinson. Willie was disappointed by this assignment. He preferred to be at the forefront of the battle where the action was. Balloon detail was boring: setting up the portable hydrogen gas generators, unspooling the telegraph wires, hefting the heavy balloon into place and securing the mooring lines. But Willie was excited to learn that the balloonist who would be ascending in the basket that he and his crew were positioning was a man from his home state of Wisconsin.

Peter Cummns wore no uniform. He, like most of the Balloon Corps, was not an enlisted man. He was attired in baggy pants tucked into high-topped boots, a woolen shirt and a slouch hat like the one favored by his boss, T. S. C. Lowe. The balloonists were civilian contractors and as such received little support (and less regard) from the regular army troops. The brigade commanders disliked these arrogant fellows who slowed down troop movements and tended to draw artillery fire from the enemy when they were aloft—canon balls that often landed uncomfortably close to the tents of the officers.

Willie and Peter had an opportunity to confab as the balloon filled with hydrogen. Their chit-chat centered around their hometowns, familiar places, friends and common acquaintances. It was inevitable that the girl with the brown hair and green eyes would become a topic of conversation. The two young men agreed that Cassie Bentley was the embodiment of beauty, charm and grace, and the most beguiling reason for surviving the war they could imagine. They did not agree upon which of them should have the right of returning, victorious and heroic, to claim the maiden's hand.

Yet this point of contention did not seem to alter the bond that was growing between them. As the thunder of the enemy bombardment and the crackle of answering rifle fire echoed through the hills, they were heartened by each others' bravado. A malevolent wind like the sound of women wailing blew through tall pines and buffeted the inflating balloon. They shared the chill.

In late June of 1862, along the Chickahominy River in Hanover County, Virginia, the second bloodiest battle of the Civil War was raging. It was the third of the Seven Days Battles as Confederate General Robert E. Lee attacked along the right flank of the Union Army. Federal troops under Brigadier General Fitz John Porter were dug in along Boatswain's Swamp. The Southern Forces greatly outnumbered those of the North, a circumstance unique in most skirmishes of the war. This particular bloodletting would become known as the Battle of Gaines' Mill.

T. S. C. Lowe's encampment was in a hollow next to a mosquito infested swamp. The good professor was deathly ill: he had contracted malaria. Brigadier General Porter requested a balloon ascension to gain information on Lee's troop placements. Lowe told Peter Cummins to go aloft in the Intrepid, the only balloon fully equipped with telegraphy. It would take an hour to inflate the Intrepid and the General was anxious. Cummins cut the bottom off of a tea kettle and attached it to another balloon, the Eagle, which was already filled with hydrogen. He funneled the gas into the Intrepid and was ready to go in only fifteen minutes.

"Come with me," Peter said to Willie Wilkinson.

"I've never been up in a balloon before," Willie replied.

"Nothing to it. You aren't afraid, are you?"

"What if they shoot us down?" Willie could hear gunfire in the distance.

"We go up one thousand feet. There's no way they can hit us with anything. Come on! Grab a rifle, just in case."

At the end of its tethering lines the balloon was indeed immune to gun fire from the ground. It had to ascend, however, to gain that altitude and on the way up it made an irresistible target for the Confederate soldiers. An artillery brigade spotted the Intrepid rising and stuffed a double charge into their Armstrong gun, angled it toward the balloon and fired. The big gun, overloaded, exploded.

"I feel just like a sitting duck up here," Willie said, crouching down below the edge of the basket.

"Take these binocular telescopes and make yourself useful," Peter told him. "See if you can spot any troop movements."

General Robert E. Lee had begun to move his forces across the Chickahominy River. Heavy canon fire erupted from the Confederate headquarters between Mechanicsville and Gaines' Mill. Willie could see a large force snaking along the banks of the river and rushed to the telegraph key. In code, he communicated to Brigadier General Fitz John Peter that an enemy column was about to outflank the Union Army on their extreme right, near the crossing at Woodbury's Bridge. Willie continued to scan the horizon using the binoculars.

"What in perdition's name is that!" he exclaimed, pointing to a large, bulging, multicolored bubble that was floating swiftly toward them.

Willie had just seen the Confederate Army's only observation balloon, the Galaxy. The Galaxy had been pieced together by Dr. Edward Cheves of Savannah, Georgia, who had bought up all the silk in Savannah and collected petticoats from Southern Belles wishing to contribute to the cause. He had made varnish from the melted-down rubber of old railroad car springs and coated the balloon with it. The balloon had originally been filled with illuminating gas from the Richmond Gas Works which had very little lifting power, much less than Lowe's hydrogen. Now on the battlefield the balloon was inflated with hot air from a stove burning pine cones soaked in turpentine. It managed to rise to one thousand feet for several hours at a time.

The Galaxy was manned by Lieutenant Captain John Randolph Bryan who had made several ascensions during the Seven Days Battle. Today, however, one of the ground crew had become entangled in the tethering lines and had cut the balloon loose. It now drifted directly toward the Intrepid.

Willie Wilkinson steadied his rifle against the top of the basket and aimed at the Confederate Balloon that was now just a few hundred feet away: an easy target for the young man who had grown up hunting quail and rabbit in the Wisconsin countryside. Willie fired, reloaded and fired again, scoring two hits on the balloon's exterior. The Galaxy slowly began to loose altitude.

When the Galaxy reached the Intrepid its colorful bulk was barely below the level of the Intrepid's hanging basket. It brushed against the tethering lines and grazed the bottom of the basket, tipping it over. Peter grabbed onto the ropes that secured the basket to the balloon but gasped as he saw Willie begin to slip out of the basket. He lunged and managed to take hold of Willie's arm stopping his progress into empty space and certain death. Now Willie was dangling dangerously over the edge.

"Grab my arm just above the wrist," Peter told him. "Now the other." Peter closed his hands around Willie's arms. He now had the kind of hold on the other man that he had learned during his days as a trapeze artist. One thousand feet below them, the ground crew rushed to drag the balloon down to earth.

As Willie swung helplessly over the edge of the basket, a troubling thought occurred to Peter. How easy it would be to release his grip and watch his rival plummet to the ground! He wouldn't be blamed for failing to save Willie, after all, he'd given it his best effort. The girl, Cassie, would be free of any obligation she might have had. Peter could approach her without interference. She would never know he had been the cause of Willie's demise. His fingers began to sweat.

*   *   *

By 1863 the Union Army Balloon Corps had been disbanded. In July of 1864 the Second Wisconsin Volunteer Infantry Regiment was mustered out. In spite of the attempts by the Confederate soldiers to riddle the balloons with rifle balls, there had been no casualties among the balloonists. The Wisconsin regiment, however, lost 10 officers, and 228 enlisted men were killed in battle, while another 77 died from disease. At the battle of Gaines' Mill there had been between 60,000 and 65,000 Confederate soldiers; the Union forces numbered about 34,000. Confederate losses, those killed, wounded, missing or captured, totaled upwards of 8,000; Union casualties were nearly 7,000.

Cassie waited at the depot as the train rolled into Delavan. She watched with dismay as several long pine boxes were unloaded: Delavan's fallen heroes had returned. By the end of the Civil War, 64 such boxes would be delivered to the small town. Mothers and fathers stood silently sobbing or crying out in anguish as the coffins, dreadful in their simplicity, were loaded onto wagons. Cassie couldn't help but add her own tears to the doleful review.

Soldiers were beginning to descend from the train car; Cassie scanned their faces. Young men who had been full of life—so many lifetimes ago—and who had beamed with the dash and appetite of the valiant when they clustered around the old oak tree to sign to fight Johnny Reb—now moved sluggishly, their faces ashen and sallow, some missing an arm or a leg, all deprived of dash and vigor. Yet there was one who retained a bit of sparkle in his tired eyes. His hair hung long and unkempt, his beard was unruly, a slouch hat sat askew on his head, a smile crept across his parched lips. The smile was for her.

Cassie returned the smile. The effect of her beaming

115

countenance was to brighten the day for the bedraggled heroes crowding the platform. A few even approached the radiant young woman—one eager man in particular. She hadn't recognized him under all that facial hair. She was startled when the man embraced her. And then, with the sudden realization that this strange, disheveled man encircling her in his arms was Peter Cummins, she returned the embrace.

"Peter! Oh, Peter! It's so good to see you!"

"I've dreamed of this moment, Cassie. The dream kept me from going insane during that awful debacle."

"Peter, is there any news of my William...Willie Wilkinson? I had hoped..."

Peter was momentarily taken back, but then realized that Cassie had been waiting for Willie, not for him. "You hadn't heard?" he said. "He's on this train."

Cassie glanced over at the coffins arrayed upon the wagons. "Is he...?"

"He's fine, Cassie. But he was wounded at Gettysburg. He's lost an arm, Cassie. And he's very down about it. Don't be surprised if he avoids you."

"Oh..."

"All he ever talked about was coming home to you. Marriage, children, all of that. But after he lost the arm..."

"It wouldn't matter. I must see him. Talk to him."

"Cassie, if it doesn't work out for you and Willie...well, you know how I feel about you."

"Oh, Peter!" said Cassie as she hugged him again. Peter leaned down, looked into her eyes, and stole a quick kiss. Just at this moment, a soldier, wearing a cap upon which was a bright medal in the shape of a hot air balloon emblazoned with the letters "BC," hobbled down the steps of the train car. He steadied himself with his single arm. When he saw Peter and Cassie in what he could only interpret as a lover's embrace, he faded quickly into the crowd and was gone.

Two weeks later, a dinner had been organized to honor the returning soldiers. The site of the dinner was the Stowell Tavern, a rambling wooden building on the west side of town which had originally been a Temperance House. Cassie volunteered to act as a server. After a sumptuous meal of wild turkey and venison, speeches and tributes, and a report by James Lawton, editor and publisher of the Delavan Republican on the latest war news, the attendees broke up into small groups of friends and relatives. Cassie had her first opportunity to talk to Willie since his return and his avoidance of her.

He turned away, but her pleading softened his reluctance. His greeting was somber, chin tucked down, eyes focused on the floor. She told him it didn't matter if he wasn't whole—she just wanted him back. He said it mattered to him—he could never take care of her this way. She asked him to give her the chance to make him happy. He asked her about Peter Cummins.

"Peter is just a friend."

"I saw you two kissing. He saved my life once, did you know that? You and he should be together. I give you my blessing."

Cassie tried to explain but Willie had walked away from her. Suddenly the dinginess of the old Temperance House closed in on her. Willie's depression and suppressed anger had taken its toll. It was if the very war itself, with invisible, icy fingers, had clutched her heart. The town took on a ghost-like pallor; the air seemed to solidify, making each breath a struggle. Yet Cassie would not surrender to despair. She resolved to break through Willie's pessimism. Now she set out upon a campaign to win him back.

Peter too was affected by Willie's melancholia. Try though he might he was unable to penetrate the gloom that enveloped the other man like a shroud. Frustrated, Peter made a mistake that threatened to bury their friendship permanently. He said, "I didn't save your life so you could throw it away. Go to the girl. You belong together." Willie's response was a chilling recrimination expressed only through a numbing glare. No words of explanation preceded Willie's exit from Peter's presence. No apology nor pleading could reel him back.

In the weeks that followed Cassie made little progress. Although Willie occasionally agreed to see Cassie, their sessions were cut short by his episodes of chest pains and shortness of breath. Randolph Wilkinson, Willie's father, brought in a specialist from Madison, a Doctor Mendes, who had treated many war veterans with similar symptoms.

"Soldier's Heart," the doctor quickly diagnosed. "There is nothing physically wrong with him, but he has all the earmarks of heart disease. We see this in soldiers who have been in the most horrific battles. They are fine one day, then cardiac neurosis strikes. We must remove him from the stress of everyday life. Loose clothing, moderate exercise, a quiet environment, rest and good diet—there's a soldiers' home just outside Madison where he could make a complete recovery. I recommend he have no visitors, however." Willie was subsequently shipped off to Doctor Mendes' sanatorium.

Dismayed by the doctor's orders of "no visitors," Cassie decided to turn to Peter Cummins for sympathy and advice. The landlady at Peter's rooming house informed her that Cummins had left some days ago for Madison where he had enlisted in the 43rd Regiment Wisconsin Volunteer Infantry, part of "The Hundred Days Men," groups of volunteers raised to swell the ranks of the Union Army in order to achieve victory—hopefully within a mere one hundred days. She was now, once again, separated from the two men in her life who had professed to love her.

*   *   *

It was October of 1864. The 43rd had moved from Nashville by train to Johnsonville to guard the railroad terminal there, a crucial link for the Union's supply trains to and from the Tennessee River. Peter Cummins had expected to see action when he enlisted. Only the sharp crack of musket fire, the boom of canon, the haunting shrill of the Rebel yell could shatter his malaise. But at Johnsonville the regiment was assigned garrison duties which, though important, were disappointingly dull.

A month later the Confederate Army attacked the gun boats stationed below the town, forcing them upriver to Johnsonville. The Rebels set up a six gun battery and began a bombardment which was answered in kind by the federal forces. The 43rd were deployed in the trenches behind the earthworks and, as this was strictly an artillery battle, were unable to engage the enemy. Adding to Peter's chagrin at being detached from the heart of the conflict was the dubious decision of the Union officers to abandon and burn the boats in order to prevent the enemy from capturing them. Gunboats, supply barges, and storage buildings were torched setting off munitions in a spectacular display of flame and fury. The description used later by journalists, that "all hell had broken loose," was never more accurate.

Willie sat on a folding chair wrapped in a heavy woolen blanket. The cold November air had whispers of winter in it as it wafted off of Lake Mendota. Behind him, half way up a gradually sloping hill sat the Queen Anne style house that served as the soldiers' home. Behind it loomed the stark, gray granite façade of Wisconsin's State Asylum for the Insane. Behind that was the Memorial Cemetery, resting place of war dead, deceased residents of Madison and the insane who had died in the asylum, some said, from a lack of proper care.

Willie was watching the "V" formation of a flock of Canadian geese circling idly over the lake, honking their goodbyes as they prepared to wing southward. They might fly as far south as the Mexican border or stay in the Midwest all winter. He had read somewhere that these geese mated for life. Mating for life...what was it about that phrase?

"It will be getting dark soon, William. Time to go in," said the woman dressed in a nurse's uniform who stood beside him looking out over the lake.

"They mate for life," he said.

"I'm sorry...what did you say?"

"The geese. They mate for life. Something I'm trying to remember. It doesn't matter."

The nurse helped Willie up the hill to the house. Doctor Mendes now had over a dozen ex-soldiers under his care. Some, like Willie, had physical injuries—all were emotionally impaired, the result of battle stress that had been held at bay through bravery, only to surface once the horrifying quiet of their homecoming fell upon them like a heavy weight.

"Doctor is letting you have a visitor this afternoon," the

nurse told Willie.

"I don't want to see anyone."

They entered the front hall and there she was. Willie stiffened. "I don't want to see anyone," he repeated.

"Please, Willie," Cassie said. "Come sit with me for a few moments, won't you?"

This was the first of many attempts Cassie would make to break through the wall that Willie had put up between himself and the outside world. They would sit silently, she sometimes voicing trivialities, anecdotes of Delavan life, obvious observations about the natural beauty of the lake— anything to elicit a reaction from him. On the rare occasions when Willie responded, his words seemed to make no sense to her.

One day he said, "I can feel my arm. The one that's missing." She looked askance at him, surprised by his statement. "It's true," he continued. "Sometimes my hand makes a fist without my having told it to do so. Sometimes the arm just aches as if I've been carrying something heavy for too long."

As incredible as that seemed, Cassie was happy that Willie had at last talked about his injury. It was a good sign. But it would be a long while before he opened up like that again. Snow heaped up along the byways and the dense fogs of winter painted the sky a dismal gray. Cassie's trips to Madison were fewer and then by January, when blizzards closed the roads, they ceased altogether.

As soon as it was possible she resumed her visits. Willie now seemed to have deteriorated. Physically he seemed to have shrunken. He had withdrawn again into a private world, perhaps where demons haunted him. He sat in silence while Cassie talked in soft tones.

Little by little Cassie began to bring him back. Now and then when she arrived at the soldiers' home, Willie appeared to brighten. However, he vocalized only nonsensical words and phrases. He repeated a name: "Danny." Cassie sought out Doctor Mendes, her curiosity piqued—was the name a key?

"Doctor Mendes," she asked, "who is Danny? Willie keeps mentioning him."

"I don't know. Maybe it was the name of a soldier in his

regiment. Maybe *the* soldier..."

"What do you mean?"

"Ah, you don't know the full story, do you? Of course not. When Willie was at Gettysburg he received the wound that later became infected, causing the amputation of his arm."

"Yes, I was aware of that."

"What you may not know is that he and another soldier, perhaps it was this Danny, were pinned down by enemy rifle fire. They were in a sort of depression, not quite a hole, where it was impossible raise their heads without getting them blown off. This went on for most of the day. Eventually the other boy panicked and stood up, ready to jump out and run. He was riddled with musket balls. Willie tried to pull him back and was shot in the arm. It must have been dreadfully traumatic."

"And you think this is the cause of his...Soldier's Heart?"

"Well, it's probably not that simple, but yes, I do."

Sometime later, when Willie seemed relatively improved, Cassie mustered the courage to ask him about Danny. At first he sat stiff as if frozen. He was staring blankly into empty space. Cassie worried that he would have another attack of heart palpitations but before she could call for the nurse Willie melted into a slump, turned toward her with tears in his eyes.

"Danny...I couldn't save him," he said. "He was in the hole. The cracks...the cracks..."

"The cracks? You mean the rifle fire?"

Willie looked at Cassie, his expression shifting from surprise to disbelief to shock. He stood and walked from the room, not looking back.

*   *   *

Peter Cummins and Cassie Bentley didn't meet again until the following year, 1866. It was a cold, mist-filled day in March and there were few buds on the trees along the ridge overlooking Lake Comus. The Spring Grove Cemetery was desolate, the effects of a harsh winter still evident. The crowd of people gathered around the new grave at the

Wilkinson plot were beginning to disperse, the ceremony having ended on some less than inspiring comments by the Reverend Lewis. Lewis had found it impossible not to allude to the religious consequences of suicide in his homily.

William Wilkinson had been sitting in the front room of the soldiers' home one year ago, nearly to the day. Cassie had sat with him, desperately trying to engage him in conversation when a large black bird, probably a crow or a raven, flew against the window with a loud crash. As long cracks spider-webbed across the window panes Willie began to scream. Doctor Mendes was only able to calm him with laudanum, a tincture of opium commonly used to relieve pain and ease the patient into a peaceful slumber.

Willie's condition did not improve and soon Doctor Mendes transferred him to the nearby asylum. Willie had alternated between catatonic trances and hysterical raving for months until Doctor Mendes, in consultation with other doctors on staff at the Wisconsin Asylum for the Insane, had moved him from the ward to an isolated room. There he languished, alone, fearful, drugged, and without hope.

Although the asylum staff had taken care to remove his belt and shoe laces, Willie fashioned a crude rope from pieces of fabric ripped from his clothing and bed sheets. There was nothing on the ceiling to loop his noose over so he tied one end of it to the bed frame, the other tightly around his neck, and managed to strangle himself in what must have been a long and agonizing death.

Cassie and Peter stood at the grave as the casket was being lowered. Besides the cemetery workers, only Willie's mother remained. Cassie looked away as the sight of that grief-stricken woman would again summon her tears. Her eyes fell upon a tombstone in the Wilkinson plot. With a shock she read the name: Daniel Wilkinson, April 20 1843, died February 2, 1848. Aloud she exclaimed, "Danny!"

Evelyn Wilkinson turned to look at Cassie. "Yes," she said. "Willie and Danny are together now."

The words which formed on Cassie's lips were not, perhaps, ones she should have uttered. "The cracks?" was all she could say. "He couldn't save him because of the cracks!"

"My child," said Evelyn Wilkinson, "you didn't know

Willie had a brother? You were too young to remember, I suppose."

"What happened? Oh, I'm sorry...I shouldn't..."

"It's all right. It was a long time ago. Willie and Danny were skating on Lake Delavan. They shouldn't have been out there...I blame myself for it! It was one of those mild winters where things freeze and then thaw and then freeze again. The ice...Danny fell through. He was struggling to get out of the freezing water but the ice kept cracking. Willie couldn't get to him. I worried that Willie would blame himself for his brother's death. It was funny though, he never cried."

*   *   *

The wind had picked up again. It blew across the small park in downtown Delavan lifting last autumn's dried leaves and twigs and swirling them like tiny tornadoes. The cobblestone walks that crisscrossed the park were filled with onlookers, anxious to see the balloon ascension. Peter Cummins, clad in purple tights and sporting a walrus style mustache, stood at the ready, trapeze bar in hand. As the great balloon filled with gas a man ran up to Cummins.

"Peter! It's too windy," he cried. Cummins was preparing to ascend with the balloon, suspended beneath it on a trapeze. He would swing and do stunts on the bar in order to impress Harry Buckley, owner of Buckley's Roman Hippodrome, and to convince the veteran circus man to add this act to his show. Peter waved the man away. "What's a little wind?" he said.

Buckley had agreed to the demonstration, feeling that balloon ascensions had no place at the circus, but intrigued with the idea of presenting a trapeze act in this unique manner. In this spring of 1874 Buckley was putting together an extravagant traveling show to rival that of P. T. Barnum's. Buckley's Roman Hippodrome would sprawl across several acres, requiring them to set up at fair grounds where there was enough space. Instead of a tent, Buckley would use a canvas wall to enclose a huge track where chariot races, processions of elephants and camels, the shenanigans of clowns and the spectacular feats of acrobats would take place. Twenty Native Americans of the Iroquois Nation would demonstrate their Indian game of Lacrosse and enact the rescue of Captain John Smith by Pocahontas.

"Your husband is a fool to ascend in this wind," Buckley said to the woman next to him.

"He won't be dissuaded," answered Cassie Cummins, the balloon ascensionist's wife.

When Cassie and Peter had left the cemetery eight years ago their courtship had begun in earnest. "I need some joy in my life," Cassie had said. "You will be the joy in mine," Peter had said. But the road to true romance had been bumpy. The girl would probably never recover from the loss of her first love. The boy still had wanderlust. Yet she became a stable factor in his life, while he sparked within her an all but smothered desire.

Perhaps because they were no longer young, perhaps because their love came not easily but through effort, a perfect union evolved. Still, it took time to evolve. Peter came and went, his interest in performing for the circus took him on the road. She would not follow. When he returned to Delavan after each tour they talked of a more sedate life. After two seasons on the road with the circus, Peter finally acquiesced. He took a job with the Hollingsworth and Bentley Livery.

Marriage and a child followed. George Bentley retired and Peter was made a partner in the business. Life was good. Then Peter heard that Harry Buckley was forming a new circus. It was too compelling. He started practicing his old act, visiting old circus friends and using their equipment. He wrote to a former member of the Balloon Corps who had been touring the country, performing ascensions. Come to Delavan, he said. The circus will welcome you.

Now the balloon was almost full. A murmur came from the crowd. Would the ascent be canceled? The wind was buffeting the big sack as if it were a child's toy. Peter stepped into the basket holding the trapeze bar that was attached by cables to the bottom of the basket. Once an adequate height was reached he would hop out and start his act. As the balloon rose the crowd cheered. Cassie let out a gasp, suddenly gripped by a premonition.

The guy wires stopped the balloon at one hundred feet, high enough to be dramatic, low enough so that the crowd could see Peter clearly. The wind had blown the balloon over the roof of the Park Hotel, and the crowd rushed around to the back of the building for a better view. Peter leaped from the basket and rode the trapeze down in a graceful arch. He pumped his feet and swung back and forth, eliciting oohs and ahs from the spectators below. He executed a 360 degree rotation around the bar, hung from his knees, reversed his position by releasing one hand after the other, and balanced on the bar on his stomach with hands and feet splayed out like a giant spider swinging from its web. He was a splendid success.

"Bring him down," yelled Harry Buckley. "It's too windy. Tell him he's got the job, but get him down from there."

The ground crew signaled to Peter and began pulling on the guy wires. Just as the balloon was about to clear the roof of the hotel the wind gusted violently and basket and suspended aerialist Peter Cummins were blown against the side of the building. Peter lost his grip and fell to the ground.

*   *   *

1904 dawned with the new century's promise of progress and prosperity still fresh on its lips. It was a leap year. There would be baseball games and a new hero named Ty Cobb, a world's fair in Saint Louis where the ice cream cone would be invented, the first airplane flight, the first construction work on the Panama Canal, a new president named Theodore Roosevelt, and Coca-Cola chewing gum. The pope would condemn low-cut woman's dresses and Mrs. Gladys Hamilton would be arrested in the newly named Times Square in New York City for smoking a cigarette in an automobile.

The circuses were all gone from Delavan, Wisconsin. The town was quiet now, the trumpeting of elephants and the clatter of wagons was no longer heard along Walworth Avenue. Circus mogul Harry Buckley now owned a hardware store downtown. On nearby Lake Delavan, where once the famous Mabie Brothers Circus had been quartered, a resort occupied the shore line. Summer cottages had appeared with boat landings and beaches, aimed at capitalizing on area's the new economy based on tourism.

Doctor Zeininger's house at Fourth and Ladd Streets sat sheltered by stately maples. His Model A Ford motorcar was parked by the curb. On the front porch, in a bentwood rocking chair, the doctor's mother-in-law watched as neighborhood children played ball in the dusty street, a shawl draped across her legs. In the kitchen, the doctor's wife, Margaret, inspected the turkey in the cast iron oven. She called to her daughter, Ellen, to come in from the garden to help with the mashed potatoes.

"And Ellen," she said when the girl had burst through the back door, "go tell your Grandma Cass that dinner will be ready in about a half hour. And slow down!"

"Yes, Mama."

Ellen Zeininger had turned sixteen last month. She enjoyed the rapport she and her grandmother had with one another. She could talk to Grandma Cass about nearly anything—girlish concerns that would make her own mother uncomfortable. Grandma Cass had a different outlook on life than did Ellen's parents.

"Dinner's almost ready, Gram," she said gently closing the screen door behind her (she had slowed down).

"Come sit with me for a bit, child. Tell me what's on your mind these days."

"Oh...nothing."

"How's your school? What's happening with your friends? Do you have a beau?"

"A beau...really, Gram!"

"You're getting to that age, Ellen. Your old Gram is full of advice whenever you're ready for it."

"I know, Gram. Gram? Tell me what happened to Grandpa...after he fell from the balloon. You never said."

"Grandpa Cummins? Oh, poor Peter! He lingered for nearly a week. All busted up. He's buried up at Spring Grove. You've seen the grave."

"Yes, but...did he suffer much? Were you by his side until the end? It's so tragic!"

"Romantic, you mean. No, it wasn't romantic at all. And me? I couldn't face it. I should have been there at his side, wiping his fevered brow, whispering loving things to him...but I just couldn't go through that again. We'd argued about his doing the balloon trick. I relented but I never should have agreed to it. Then there was that wind...that horrible wind! They all told him not to do it. But he had to prove something, I guess.

"When they brought him home and the doctor said there was nothing he could do...I sort of went into shock. I turned away from it all. Ask your mother, she was there. She saw. I just sat in the parlor the whole time, staring out the window. Wouldn't talk to anybody, wouldn't help out. I was like I was made of stone. At the funeral I didn't cry. I didn't cry all that year and most of the next. Then, one day, I was sitting, looking out the window as usual. A large bird flew against the window knocking itself out. All of a sudden, all the tears I'd held back for so long came like a flood. I became hysterical and cried for hours. Nobody saw that, thank God."

"Oh, Gram, that's so sad."

"I guess it's strange the way emotions come and go like that. Well, now you know the whole story. I wonder if there is anything to be learned from it."

"Gram? I do have a beau. Well, sort of a beau. He's very handsome and I think he likes me."

"I thought as much. Do you want some advice? Don't let him join the army, work for the circus, or go up in a balloon!"

THE LOST PRINCE OF GREEN BAY

A Telltale Heart Finds Its Place in History

By Anne Swardson
Washington Post Foreign Service
Thursday, April 20, 2000

PARIS, April 19—The fate of Louis XVII of France, a royal heir lost in the blood and flames of revolution, has been one of Europe's most intriguing and enduring historical mysteries, spawning hundreds of books and dozens of pretenders to the French throne for more than two centuries.

The mystery finally ended today: DNA analysis confirmed that the heart of the young king rests in a crystal globe in a basilica in a suburb of Paris. Experts said that the evidence provided by the telltale heart offers scientific proof that Louis-Charles, the son of King Louis XVI and Queen Marie-Antoinette, both guillotined during the French Revolution, died shortly thereafter at the age of 10, ending a theoretical two-year reign as Louis XVII.

Gordon threw down his newspaper, nearly spilling the coffee that teetered precariously in its paper cup. "Ha! I told you so," he said, a smug smile creeping across his face.

"Yes, I've read it," I replied. "Still, I have problems with the conclusions...I should say, assumptions that were made in the service of propriety."

David Gordon and I were often found at one of the small

tables at the Starbucks on Oneida Street in Ashwaubenon, Wisconsin, a suburb of Green Bay—or of the Oneida Nation, depending on who you talked to. Of the several subjects we would bandy about as we relaxed, sipped lattes and read the national papers, our favorites were conspiracy theories, each of us taking pro or con alternately. It was my turn to argue for the conspiracy side. Gordon began his defense:

"Jack, they took five different samples from the heart: four from the epicardium of the wall and one from the ascending aorta. They used two independent labs in Germany and in Belgium. They agreed..."

"They were testing for mitochondrial DNA, according to this article. That tries to trace ancestry back through the mother's line. You need a perfect match to indicate a link, not just a 'probable one.' They couldn't possibly be sure..."

"They had locks of hair from Marie-Antoinette herself and from her two sisters. The hair had been stored in lockets that were in the Paris Musées. And look, it says here that 'two living descendants of the sisters, Queen Anna of Romania and her brother, Andre of Bourbon-Parma, donated tissue samples for comparison.' Surely that is definitive?"

"David, think about it. There was a rumor that the child, Louis-Charles, who became the Dauphine and then Louis XVII, wasn't even fathered by Louis XVI. There was a count, Count Axel von Fersen, who was thought to be the father."

"So what? It's the mother's lineage that we are looking at."

"And these locks of hair? How do we know they came from Marie-Anoinette?"

"There are inscriptions on the backs of the lockets. It was a common practice to give locks of hair as gifts."

"I know another story about her hair, David. When she tried to escape from Paris during the revolution—it is said that her hair turned white."

"Well, the article doesn't say what the origin of the hair used was or what color it was. The executioner supposedly cut her hair so the guillotine blade would sever her neck cleanly. The legend is that he stuffed her hair in his pocket. Maybe it came from that."

"So," I said, and realizing that this conversation would call for a second latte, I jumped up to order two more. "And so," I continued when I returned to the table, "let us turn to the heart of Louis XVII. Its provenance troubles me."

David Gordon is what you'd call a 'big man,' being well over six feet tall and weighing nearly 200 pounds. I am only five foot ten and a lean 142 pounds, making the sight of the two of us together fairly comical, like the old funny papers couple, Mutt and Jeff. Only we lack the mustaches and I do have a full head of hair. I thought about this physical difference and about the disparity between our chosen professions: he, an insurance agent and I, a self-proclaimed folk artist. Well, perhaps I would be better described as a folk who did art. My wood carvings are featured in galleries across the state, but had I not a substantial inheritance, I would qualify instead for the descriptive title of 'starving artist.' But I digress. Gordon began again:

"Louis XVI and Marie-Antoinette went to the guillotine in the year 1793. The young prince, now technically the King of France (although the monarchy had been abolished by the French Revolution), was sent to the Temple prison where he eventually contracted tuberculosis and died. The doctor doing the autopsy removed his heart and it was stored in the basilica of St. Denis until the present day when samples were taken from it for the DNA testing."

Gordon was up on his history. Like myself, anticipating the debate that would ensue between us, he had researched the story of the Lost Prince. The newspaper article about the DNA tests had appeared two days ago—plenty of time for a trip to the library or the use of a search engine to explore the internet.

"Yes, that is true," I replied. "The ten year-old boy was kept in a cold dark cell and, they say, abused badly. He was later attended to by a couple named Simon. The Simons were able to stop the guards from beating the poor child and they treated him with compassion. Some say they rescued him."

"Ha! Here is where your conspiracy theory takes fruit, I'll wager. A conspiracy to rival that of the Grand Duchess Anastasia or John F. Kenedy!"

"The Simons quit their job suddenly. There were rumors

at the time that the prince had disappeared and that Simon had smuggled him out in a laundry basket, substituting a deaf and dumb boy he had found on the streets."

"The Prince and the Pauper."

"Well, not exactly, although Mark Twain did write about *our* Lost Dauphin in Huckleberry Finn."

"You mean Eleazer Williams, of course."

"I'll get to him in a minute. Anyway, the conspiracy theory, as you call it, does begin with Simon. He was later guillotined and his wife swore that the story was true. They had rescued the prince. And the doctor who did the autopsy, died suddenly. Was he killed so he couldn't reveal that the dead boy wasn't the prince?"

"Better and better. It's like JFK being hidden away on the Aristotle Onassis yacht."

"Twenty years later the body of the boy who had died in the Temple prison—whoever he was—was exhumed to be moved to the royal sepulcher, but the grave was found to be empty. And the heart that was supposed to belong to Louis XVII..."

"Oh...here we go," said Gordon, swirling his latte and giving me one of those incredulous looks of his that I so love to elicit.

"Here, I've written it down from my research." I read from my notes:

"Philippe-Jean Pelletan was the name of the physician who did the autopsy. He admitted in a hand written document that still exists, that he removed the heart from the dead boy and secretly took it, wrapped in a handkerchief and stuffed into his pocket. It was kept in a glass case on his bookshelf, preserved in alcohol. The alcohol later dried up. It was stolen in 1810 by a student, Jean-Henri Tillos, who subsequently died of tuberculosis. His wife returned it to the doctor.

"In 1828, Dr. Pelletan, perhaps feeling guilty about retaining his illicit souvenir, gave the heart to the archbishop of Paris. It remained with the archbishop in its crystal case until the Revolution of 1830. An angry mob had stormed the archbishop's residence and carried off various items, including the heart. At this point we have the evidence of a B. Lescroart who tried to rescue the heart and wrestled with another revolutionist for it. But the case shattered and the heart was lost.

"Two days later, Lescroart led Pelletan's son to the scene of the struggle and together they searched for the heart. They found glass shards scattered across the archbishop's courtyard. They then recovered the heart which had been buried under a pile of sand. You can imagine the condition of that vital organ by this time. Pelletan then turned the heart over to the Bourbon Heirs of France who, because of the revolution, now had no royal standing whatsoever. It wasn't until 1975 that the heart again resurfaced, this time to join other royal relics at the basilica of St. Denis."

"Seems like the trail is well documented. And how do you explain the DNA match between the heart and the locks of hair?"

"I don't. If in fact the heart that ended up at St. Denis was the same heart removed from the boy who died in prison—and it changed hands so many times that we just cannot be certain—the condition that it must have been in would have precluded any accurate DNA samples."

"They get good results from mummies, thousands of years old. Why not from this?"

"Too many convenient assumptions. Provenance of the heart and of the hair is muddled. Could have been the heart belonging to Louis Joseph Xavier François, the older brother and the original Dauphin. And weren't there two daughters? Could have been from some other relative."

"Well, you haven't convinced me," Gordon said, carrying his empty cup to the trash receptacle. "I've got to get back to the office."

We hadn't had time to discuss that other aspect of the story that so piqued my own interest—the story's link to Green Bay, Wisconsin: Eleazer Williams, the King Without a Crown, the Lost Dauphin. I decided to drive to the Oneida Reservation where Eleazer Williams was buried at the Church of the Holy Apostles, the oldest Indian mission of the Episcopal Church and where Williams had become its first missionary in 1821.

I stood before the simple marker in the shade of an ancient oak, contemplating the man whose remains were there beneath the earth. There were no flowers although the grave itself had been well kept by the grounds keeper. Eleazer Williams, born May, 1788, somewhere near Lake George, New York State, had been baptized Razar Williams although his Indian name was Onwarenhiiaki, which means "his head has been split," (an apt appellation given the duality of persona which dominated his later life). He was a chief of Caughnawaga reserve and a Congregational and Episcopal minister.

He was the son of Thomas Williams, also a chief of the Caughnawaga, whose Indian name was Tehoragwanegen, and Mary Ann Rice, whose Indian name was Konwatonteta. Eleazer would later claim that the Williams were not his natural parents, but had adopted him; that he had been brought to America from France at an early age and given into the care of the Indian tribe. He told the story that at age thirteen he had dived into the lake and struck his head resulting in amnesia. He could remember nothing of his earlier life and assumed he was of Native American lineage like the other children on the reservation.

He and his brother, John, were sent for an education to Massachusetts where they entered a Congregational school and soon he aspired to the Congregational ministry in spite of the opposition of his devout Catholic mother. When he and his brother returned to New York the War of 1812 was raging. Eleazer would claim to have participated in that war, being given the title of Superintendent General of Indian Affairs, and claim he had helped win the Battle of Plattsburgh through clever strategy of his own invention, although there is no record of any this.

After the war he switched denominations and became an Episcopal minister. This church, in 1815, was the American equivalent of the Anglican Church of England and was very invested in Christianizing the indigenous peoples of the New World. William was fluent in Mohawk and integrated well with the Oneidas of New York State. He was influential in converting most of the Oneidas to Christianity and began lobbying to move the tribe to a new reservation in Wisconsin.

Eleazer Williams had a dream: all the Indian races living in the United States should be gathered together and form one vast united community and those not yet civilized, living as savages at odds with the inevitable plunder of their native lands by the whites, could be saved in body as well as in spirit—in the new promised land of Wisconsin.

The Oneidas were granted a tract of land near Green Bay and Williams established himself there as their spiritual leader. He married a 14 year-old Menominee girl named Madeleine Jourdain who was engaged to another man. The man happened to be out of town at the time Williams asked her father for her hand in marriage. Madeliene was informed of her prescribed marriage the following day as she prepared to leave for school.

Williams began to neglect the Oneidas, rarely visiting them at Duck Creek near Green Bay. This caused a rift between him and his flock which would eventually result in the Episcopal Bishop banning him from representing the church in Wisconsin. He moved to land that his wife had inherited along the Fox River and became increasingly disenchanted with his own Native American ancestry. During this time something happened to Eleazer Williams which led to his claim that he was the true and rightful heir to the French monarchy—that he was, in fact, the lost Prince of France, Louis XVII.

I shuffled through fallen leaves and overgrown grass as I made my way to the older part of the cemetery. There was another grave I wished to visit there among the tipped and broken markers, one almost weathered beyond the point that its epitaph could be deciphered. But I was familiar with the identity of the occupant that lay beneath the unkempt plot that smelled of damp earth and mold and decay. I traced my fingers across the letters: Herbert Lucrèce, 1785 – 1839.

David Gordon and I met for coffee the following day. I would now argue against the possibility that Eleazer Williams was the lost prince of France. We enjoyed switching positions in our debates as it kept our passions in check and exercised our brain cells. Besides, I was certain that Eleazer Williams had been a fraud. I had a personal reason to believe so.

"There is the fact," Gordon offered in argument, "that

Prince de Joinville, the son of Louis Phillip, the reigning king of France, traveled to America in 1841 for the express purpose of investigating Eleazer's claim to the throne. Why would he go to the trouble if there wasn't some evidence for the possibility? After all, there were many dozens of pretenders who made the same claim."

"Just being thorough," I explained.

"Williams gave his account of his meeting the prince by chance on the steamer Columbia sailing on Lake Michigan. He said the prince was startled when he first laid eyes on Williams. Williams apparently had a strong family resemblance to the Bourbons. The prince told him he was the lost heir but wanted him to sign a paper abdicating the throne. Williams refused."

"Yet the story, according to Prince de Joinville himself, was that he had come to America only because he was interested in the Native American culture and Williams forced the 'chance' meeting by boarding the boat in advance of their scheduled meeting."

"Williams was able to recognize a portrait in a book of Simon the Shoemaker, his former guard. And he had a mark on his shoulder, a cicatrix in the shape of a crescent that was old and nearly healed over. Francus Vinton wrote about this scar in an article for Putnam's Magazine in 1868. It was proof, he maintained, that Williams was the Dauphin."

"Putnam's was partly responsible for Eleazer Williams' fame—and those articles didn't hurt their circulation, either. The first one, I think, was by John Halloway Hanson in 1853. It was entitled, 'Have we a Bourbon among us?' And who wouldn't want that to the true? Yet Hanson, you know, was an Episcopalian colleague of Reverend Williams. Not a neutral party, I should say."

"His mother signed a document that stated that Eleazer was adopted, not her natural son. He was the only one of the children that bore no resemblance to her or her husband."

"He either tricked her into signing it or forged her name. She later denied that he was adopted. She was mortified that he had rejected her in favor of his supposed royal blood."

"It is true he had many detractors. He was forced out of the ministry and spent his last years living alone in a small cottage back in the east. He died in 1858 without there being any resolution to the issue."

"There is one more point I'd like to make about Williams," I said. "But I think we'll need more coffee again."

This round was on Gordon. As he went to the counter I sat wondering exactly how much I should tell him. After all, this was just a game, wasn't it? A mental sparing that we indulged in the way some men might play basketball in their driveways or poker in their smoke-filled rec rooms. It didn't really matter who won the debate. No one was going to assume the throne of France—not in this century anyway.

The hissing of the espresso machine and the pop music album they were playing combined with traffic sounds from outside in the driveway of the little strip mall. It all became a sort of "white noise" that blended together to buffer one from the bustle of the world outside. The white noise and that aroma of freshly brewed coffee, so addictive and stimulating, were the ambiance of choice for Gordon and myself in our endeavor to best each other intellectually.

"Yes, yes," he said, placing the two Grande Caffè Lattes on the table. "Go on with your last word—and make it good!"

"Well," I said, blowing across the paper cup and watching the foam swirl toward one side, "Williams was exhumed in 1947 and his body brought back to Green Bay for burial. At the time his bones were brought here they were laid out and arranged in proper anatomical order and photographed, and *measured*. The skull was determined to be consistent with that of someone of Native American descent."

"That sounds very scientific, Jack. But I don't think it trumps the scar or the visit from Prince de Joinville."

"Why do you suppose this man who had so much invested in Christianizing the Indians—his own people—suddenly decided he was a lost prince of France?"

"The chance meeting with de Joinville, of course."

"Williams had made the claim as early as 1839. To the editor of the Buffalo Express. That's two years earlier.

Something happened around then that gave Williams the idea."

"And what do you propose it was that happened in 1839 that influenced the Reverend Eleazer Williams to pretend to the throne of France?"

I hadn't intended to let the debate trap me into revealing the actual truth of the matter. It wasn't my place to tell it. But the passion, if there can be said to be passion in argument for argument's sake, drew me into an admission I was loath to make. I should have taken Huck Finn's advice when he said "...these liars warn't no kings nor dukes at all, but just low-down humbugs and frauds. But I never said nothing, never let on; kept it to myself; it's the best way; then you don't have no quarrels, and don't get into no trouble." But I didn't.

"Have you ever heard of Herbert Lucrèce?" I asked.

"No, never. Who is he?"

"The story starts in 1795 at the Paris Temple. Simon the Shoemaker and his wife smuggled a ten year-old boy out of the prison hidden in a laundry basket. It was part of a plot by Royalists to rescue the Dauphin and restore the monarchy at some future time. But Paris was too dangerous and filled with spies who surely would uncover the plot. So the boy was whisked away to Canada. He arrived in Sault St. Louis, Quebec where he was placed under the care of a Jesuit priest named Andre Lucrèce.

"The French Jesuits, you may remember, were established all over North America by the eighteenth century. Father Jacques Marquette and the explorer Louis Jolliet had traveled up and down the Mississippi River and as early as 1667 the Jesuits had established a mission near Green Bay for the Illiniwek Indians. Father Lucrèce was sent to Green Bay around the year 1815 and brought his young charge with him.

"The boy, who was in reality Louis-Charles de France, the son of Louis XVI and Marie-Antoinette, and therefore the present king of France, was not ready to be presented to the world by his protectors. He had adopted the name Herbert Lucrèce after that of his guardian. His identity was kept secret because his life was in danger from certain members of the revolution who had learned of his escape and sought to eliminate this last living Bourbon.

"Herbert married a local woman named Mary Steward. They had one child, a girl, named Eleanor. Herbert revealed his secret to his wife who wrote about it in her journal. The journal is in private hands and has never been made public. Now the story gets more interesting: around 1821 when Eleazer Williams came with 150 Oneida Indians to the Green Bay area..."

"Let me guess. You're going to tell me that Eleazer Williams met this Herbert Lucrèce and got the idea to pretend to be the lost Dauphin from him."

"I don't know that for sure, but Lucrèce died in 1839 from influenza. That's the same year Williams contacted George Haskins in Buffalo and began his claim to being the lost prince."

"And you know all this how? You said the journal was in private hands."

"It is. It was passed down through several generations from the daughter, Eleanor Lucrèce, who married a Bernard Hopkins..."

"Wait a minute...Hopkins? That's your name. Don't tell me you are related to..."

"Herbert Lucrèce was my great-great-great-great grandfather. I am his only living ancestor. *I* am the rightful heir to the throne of France!"

BARNUM'S GOLD

Some one of these days I'll go get it," Joey says, stirring the yolks of his over-easy eggs with a bread crust. Joey Benuto and the man opposite him in the little diner booth, one Gabriel Benning, have been working odd construction jobs around Rolla, Missouri, all summer. They've just been laid off, which suits them just fine and they've dragged their mosquito ravished bodies into Pete's Diner to celebrate their liberation with a good, for once, breakfast.

"What I don't get," says Gabe, "is why you're so all fire sure this story is true."

"'Cause it was told me by my daddy, who was told by his daddy, who heard it first hand from one of the robbers as he laid dyin'!"

"He's dyin' so's he don't tell no lies, I guess."

"That's right. The two was squashed by elephants."

"Huh?"

"They was circus. They was working with the Barnum Bailey when this big elephant gets loose and runs 'em down. Took 'em about three days to kick off. Meanwhile my granddaddy is tending to them, see. And the one fellow admits they stole Barnum's gold."

Gabe is mopping up gravy with his last biscuit. Greasy gray dribble coats a day's growth of blond chin stubble. When the biscuit is gone he drags a finger through the remaining puddle on his plate, licks, then wipes the sticky digit against dungarees already speckled with dirt, oil stains, the remains of last night's dinner of beans and pork chops, and some spots resembling bird droppings which are probably just splatters of white wash from a recent job site.

"Okay," says Gabe, "so's this P. T. Barnum is drivin' his buggy loaded with gold and they...say! Why is he drivin' along with all this gold, anyway?"

"Barnum paid his circus people in gold, you see. He took in paper money and had to exchange it up at the bank. So he's coming back from the bank and these two fellows jump out of the bushes, wearing bandanas pulled up so's only they eyes showed. That's why he don't recognize them."

"They worked for Barnum?"

"That's right. They throw Barnum off the rig and take off with the horse and buggy and the gold. But Barnum gets to this farm house and they get to the cops and the cops get after these guys pretty quick."

"P. T. Barnum, huh? Say, isn't he the guy what said 'A sucker is born every minute?'"

"No. What he actually said was, 'Every cloud has a silver lining.' Anyway, they figured they was being chased so they threw the gold into this lake up by where the circus stayed during winter, up in Wisconsin. They figured they'd come get it when the heat died down. They kept on working with the circus 'cause then they wouldn't be suspected. Then the elephant stomped on 'em."

"Tough luck. So how's come your granddaddy never went and got the gold out of that lake?"

"He looked for it. Wasn't where the fellow said, near shore by a big willow. My daddy went up there too. No luck, him. I think I know why, though. I'll tell you why. See, there's two lakes up there with almost the same name. One is called Como and the other, Comus. I think they looked in the wrong lake."

Sally, the diner's only waitress, rust colored hair bouncing, starched skirts making a sound like the scratching of baby rodents, plops a metal coffee pot onto the table. "More coffee, sweetie?" she asks.

"Thank you, darlin'," says Joey. Neither participant in this conversational ritual particularly likes being called sweetie or darlin' but they haven't much to say to each other otherwise. Gabe shakes a "no thanks" at Sally. "Where ya'll headin' next?" she asks.

"Maybe Illinois," says Joey, pronouncing the "s" like a "z". "Maybe..."

"Maybe a lake up in Wisconsin!" Gabe responds. Joey has just slurped up a mouthful of hot coffee which he promptly sprays across the table in Gabe's direction. This sudden acknowledgement of the veracity of the lost gold story by his usually doubtful friend unnerves Joey, gives him pause to consider how much he, himself, believes the tale. Makes him want to find out.

"Too hot for ya, sweetie?" asks Sally.

*   *   *

It *is* hot…unseasonably hot for October 1931, especially for Southern Wisconsin. Yet breezes that lift and twist the ruddy orange and burnt red maple leaves also skim and ruffle majestic Lake Como, borrowing its purity and coolness if only momentarily, and thereby giving the two men some relief from their day long task of rowing, rowing, rowing. They are now drifting idly, having completed two circuits of the shore line, investigating the bank near each weeping willow. There have been many of these stately trees, wispy branches caressing the water, tiny leaves windblown like wings torn from dragonflies. At each drooping tree the men have probed the lake bottom with their oars, hoping for the solid contact of a rusted strongbox but only sinking into sucking mud and scattering angry carp.

"I sure am gettin' thirsty," says Gabe, leaning back against the grimy stern of the old wooden rowboat. "I sure could use a cold beer."

"Ain't you heard of prohibition, you lunkhead?"

"Aw, Joey, this is Wisconsin…the back woods…the lairs and hidey holes of rumrunners and bootlickers."

"Bootleggers. And yes, I think there *is* a place. See that big hotel across the bay? There's a speakeasy in the basement. I heard, anyway. I guess we can call it day and go see what's what."

"A day? Hell! Is that all it's been? Okay. Your turn to row," says Gabe, who knew all along about the speakeasy at the Lake Como Hotel. He's pretty sure he's smarter than he looks, and certainly smarter than he will ever let Joey know about.

*   *   *

There had been a girl, but she had died. Joey and Gabe, eighteen and nineteen respectively, first met each other working in the girl's father's grape orchards along the old highway west of Rolla. Prohibition had been an unexpected boon for the vineyards of central Missouri: it seemed people were drinking a lot of grape juice. There was cultivating and pruning, planting, and harvesting for those not afraid of hard work. Hauling baskets of grapes to market was the boys' favorite part of the job as often Cynthia would squeeze between them in the cab, her bare legs pressing against theirs as the truck rocked and swayed along the road. Cynthia liked going to town and once the grapes were unloaded at the Frisco Line's railway terminal, the three were free to kick up their heels.

On one such heel kicking they had scored a jug of Ozark mountain moonshine and decided to stop at the Big Piney Creek near Devil's Elbow on the way home. The road dipped deep between sandstone bluffs, paralleling the river before crossing it as a steel-trussed bridge. The bridge was paved with wooden planks that rumbled as Route 66 traffic crept along it. Tall sycamores, burr oak and shortleaf pine lined the river banks where they pulled the truck off the road onto rough gravel. Upstream they could see an old railroad trestle towering above the Big Piney. At the sharp bend in the river, the Devil's Elbow, as it was named, they spread a tarp from the truck at the water's edge. The jug was uncorked and passed, and the three, who were not quite lovers but more than just friends, settled down to watch dragon flies skimming the greenish muck that swirled in eddies and to listen to the pulsing songs of cricket frogs.

Joey and Gabe later remembered they had each told Cynthia that they loved her dark hair and brown eyes and were pledged to protect her from evil as long as they lived.

"Here, have another pull from the jug."

She had responded that she loved the both of them and that they would journey through life together, always faithful and true.

"That certainly is good moonshine!"

They were all shy of twenty and had not yet ventured beyond verbal lovemaking. Not that there was any mystery in that regard. Perhaps Joey and Gabe were a bit wary of each other's potential rivalry once that stage was reached. Perhaps Cynthia wasn't willing to choose between her two beaus. Perhaps they were just not in a hurry, preferring to savor the anticipation, preserving in their imaginations a miraculous union of souls sanctified by sex.

Nevertheless, Joey and Gabe were nonplussed to watch as Cynthia kicked off her shoes, stripped off her blouse and stepped out of her shorts to stand splendid in bra and panties on the banks of the Big Piney Creek. She had just said "Come on, boys," or "What are you waiting for," or something of that nature—they couldn't remember later when they tried to analyze their actions, or rather, their inactions. They sat with open mouths as Cynthia plunged into the river, was caught by the current and carried downstream toward the confluence of the Big Piney and the Gasconade River.

*   *   *

Now on Lake Como in Wisconsin, they dock at the hotel's double pier, a forked-tongue-like affair riddled with wood rot, its two prongs poking obscenely into the placid lake. The hotel itself once was the Danish Pavilion at the 1893 Columbian Exposition and World's Fair in Chicago. Built in Denmark, transported to Chicago, then, after the fair closed, shipped to Wisconsin to the shores of Lake Como. There the building had been an ice house, then the headquarters for a hunting and fishing club, and now it is a hotel, restaurant and speakeasy. It is also, and here's something Gabe does not yet know, the summer get-away for the gangsters, Bugs Moran, Baby Face Nelson and various members of the John Dillinger gang, their wives, sweethearts, et al.

As they climb the embankment to the hotel Gabe asks, "What do we tell them we were doing if they ask?"

"Tell them we were fishing," answers Joey.

The hotel reeks of age, like an elderly aunt presiding over a funeral. The parquet floor creaks under their muddy boots. A heavy set man wearing a bright green vest and yellow bow tie descends from an ornately carved wooden staircase. "Hello, gentlemen," he says. "I'm Harold Hansen, proprietor here abouts. What can I do for you?"

"Well sir,' answers Joey, "we're a mite thirsty."

Hansen cocks his head, gives the two men a once and a twice over. What have you been doing out on the lake all day," he asks. "You sure haven't been fishing."

"We was looking for...ouch!" Gabe has been foot stomped. Joey takes over the conversation.

"We are conducting a survey of the shore line of your beautiful lake. Measuring the water depth, you see. We work for the county."

"Uh huh. Well, usually I don't ask so many questions. I've learned not to bother our illustrious guests with such trivialities. I was just curious. So, I guess you'll be interested in the Sewer?"

"The Sewer?"

"Downstairs. You can get a drink there. That is, if you're not cops or feds or friends of old Scarface Al Capone."

"No, we're from Miz-zer-ah. Don't know no one from Chicago."

"That's good," says the here-abouts proprietor, pulling at his vest. "By the way, last summer I had to dump some slots into the lake when certain people got too nosey. If you come across them, there's probably a bunch of nickels there if they haven't rusted away. Appreciate knowing if you come by them."

"We sure will let you know about that. Yes, Sir!"

"Okay. Good. You see that phone booth?" They nod. "Go in there and dial 715. It'll open to the stairs down to the Sewer."

Joey and Gabe squeeze into the phone booth which is a small closet containing a bench on which sits a candlestick telephone. Joey lifts the earpiece and twists the finger wheel dialing the numbers 7, 1 and 5. There is a sharp clack and the back wall of the closet swings open to reveal a rickety staircase leading downward. The Sewer? At least there isn't any stench of sewage, only the faint aroma of mildew, cigar smoke and booze. Down they go into the gloom, and finding yet another door, they bang on it with intense anticipation.

A little window slides open, a pair of gray-green eyes squint menacingly out at them. A blink or two, then after a moment, a bolt is thrown and they are ushered into the speakeasy known locally as "The Sewer."

Cab Calloway's "Minnie the Moocher" is playing on a Wurlitzer, colored lights flashing red, orange, and blue up the sides and across the arched top of the spectacularly gaudy jukebox. Slot machines line the quarry stone walls on one side of the long, dimly lit, cavernous room. A polished mahogany bar complete with bright brass rail dominates the opposite wall. There are round, felt covered gaming tables and a massive oak pool table where two men are leaning, cues in hand, contemplating a complicated shot involving the position of a shiny black eight ball. Smoke hangs heavily in the air like a low ceiling, broken here and there by the green shades of hanging lamps. Four men sit at one of the tables playing cards. They barely glace up as Joey and Gabe enter.

Joey and Gabe stand at the bar. Joey orders a shot of whiskey with a beer chaser. Gabe asks for a gin. The bartender pours both drinks from the same bottle, then draws the beer, neglecting to bleed off the initial foam that issues from the tap. "That's only half a glass," complains Joey receiving what is essentially a glass of foam. The bartender merely stares, eyes beginning to disappear behind lowering lids, fists and teeth clenching. Gabe, who is smarter than he looks, says, "I'll take that one. Pour my friend here another, if you please."

*   *   *

As Cynthia was swept along through Devil's Elbow and beyond, she laughed and screamed with delight. When she bobbed out of sight around the bend, Joey and Gabe panicked, mistaking her jubilance for terror. They bounded through blackberry brambles and bush honeysuckle, tripping over the exposed roots of salt cedar and box elder. Their progress was slow, obstructed by thick brush along the shore. The river's edge dropped off in muddy slopes offering no passage close to the raging torrent. They could no longer hear Cynthia's screams; the only sound was the rush of water against rock, the Big Piney taunting them with its brutal laughter.

At last the river widened, slowed, relented from its mad deluge. A sand bar bracketed a silent pool bypassed by the main current. In this stagnant liquid shelter floated a shape: unrecognizable from the distance between it and the two frantic boys. It seemed a shapeless blue-white blob encircled by dark, ropelike strands. The strands writhed, coiling, then uncoiling, then moved off.

Just one cotton-mouthed water moccasin's bite could be fatal. Three or four inflicted an eternity of pain experienced in seconds, sweet oblivion its only release. By the time Joey and Gabe reached her, Cynthia was beyond help, puffed and bloated and engraving an image of absolute horror onto memories they would never shake.

*   *   *

"Set 'em up again," says Gabe. "You've got to let me try to win some of that back." Gabe has been shooting pool with one of the men in The Sewer and has lost two games in a row. At ten bucks a game, Gabe is out nearly all the money that he and Joey had between them. The other man grins a scurrilous grin and says, "You got the dough?"

"I got plenty. Make it interesting. A hundred bucks."

"What? I don't see you as having no hundred bucks."

This exchange is piquing the interest of the table of card players. A round-faced man wearing a vest and polka dotted tie turns to watch. Joey leans against the wall, arms folded, trying to emulate the "great stone face" of Buster Keaton. He knows what is coming.

"We know where Barnum's gold is stashed. That's what we're doing up here. Came to get it. It'll more than back the bet."

"Gold? What gold?" Gabe provides a short version of the story, leaving out the location of the lake. The pool shooter is incredulous but looks over at the card players. There is a nod from the round-faced man. The terms are agreed upon: one hundred dollars against a share in the gold. And so the game begins.

Gabe wins the break and sets up the balls, pulling back

slightly on the triangle to pack the balls tightly. He twists a piece of blue chalk against the tip of his cue, taking his time. He then leans over the table, pulling slowly back on the cue, and, with a deft flick of his wrist, slams the cue ball into the rack of balls scattering them and sinking three of them. He smiles. "It's all in the wrist," he says.

The rest of the game lasts only about ten minutes as Gabe calls, then sinks shot after shot. Three ball in the side pocket. Five ball in the corner pocket. Combination shot, the six and the ten in the side pockets. Finally, only the eight ball remains. Gabe banks the cue ball off the side cushion and knocks the eight ball into a corner pocket. He has cleared the table without allowing his opponent a single shot.

"You bastard! You crumby bastard!" yells the man. Cue raised over his head, he starts toward Gabe. Gabe picks up the cue ball and winds up as if he is about to strike out Lou Gehrig.

"Hold it!" shouts the round-faced man and the two adversaries freeze. There is something in the belligerence of his manner that commands, if not respect, rapt attention. "You, give him a C-note. You lost."

"But Bugs, he hustled me. I just wanna rough him up a little."

"If there's anybody roughin' up anybody else, I'll be the one roughin' up him. You lost, fair and square. Shoulda knowed better." The round-faced man who is called "Bugs" gestures to Gabe. "You, come over here. Your buddy too. Sit!"

They sit. Bugs Moran has waved the other players away from the table. He crouches down in his chair, signaling Joey and Gabe to move in closer. "Now let's you an' me talk about this gold," he says.

*　　*　　*

Once they had carried Cynthia's body back to the truck and covered her with the tarp, they sank to the ground anguished and fearful. What could they do but return to the vineyard, weighted down with guilt and remorse. Compassion and understanding would not await them there, certainly not in the form of the girl's father. They could hide the corpse and run, making matters worse. That wasn't who they were, no sir. They'd face up to it, take the blame for what was a terrible, terrible accident, an accident they couldn't have prevented...or could they? It was their idea to stop at the Devil's Elbow. They had procured the jug of moonshine. They hadn't stopped her from plunging into the Big Piney, hadn't pulled her out in time. They were going to hell. Might as well get it over with.

They were back on the highway. Here it was called "Teardrop Road" after the notorious "Trail of Tears" along which thousands of Cherokee died during relocation in the nineteenth century. They drove through St. Robert and Waynesville, through Buckhorn where the road dips south along rolling hills with orchards of fruit trees and fields full of grapes.

Joey and Gabe shed their own trail of tears as they approached the Amarone Vineyards and Cynthia's home. They stopped the truck at the main house and waited while Mr. Amarone was sent for. "We'd better carry her inside," said Joey.

Carefully they lifted her swollen body, still wrapped in the dirty tarp and carried it through the front door. They laid her on the davenport and water smelling of algae dripped onto the floor. Rufus, the Amarones' golden retriever, entered the room, sniffed the sadness in the air, and raised his muzzle in an agonized howl that sent razor sharp shivers up their spines.

*　　*　　*

"This P. T. Barnum's gold," says Bugs, "It's like the Lost Dutchman's Mine, right?"

"No, Sir, it's a fact," says Joey.

"Well, I don't believe it for a minute. However, I like you boys. You, Mr. Pool Stick, you got a style I like. And you... well...I guess you're part of the deal. I like the way you stuck it to Wally, Mr. Pool Stick. He's an idiot, anyway."

"It's Gabe. And this is Joey. And there really is some gold." As soon as he says this, Gabe regrets insisting on the truthfulness of his story. He knows who Bugs Moran is. He knows he is a ruthless criminal, a killer, the arch rival of Al Capone and the only survivor of the Capone engineered "Saint Valentine's Day Massacre." He knows Moran runs the rackets on the North Side of Chicago. He knows Moran doesn't run broads like Capone does and considers himself a good Catholic, but booze and gambling are his forte. And killing.

"You know why they call me 'Bugs'?"

Joey maintains his great stone face. Gabe shakes his head no. Bugs continues: "'Cause sometimes I go a little crazy, see. Like when I get unhappy about somethin'. You follow me?" They both nod.

"We were just..."

"Times is rough, right?" says Bugs. "You boys need work, I bet. Can you drive?"

"We can drive."

Bugs motions to a man standing at the bar. He joins them at the table. "This is my pal, Jimmy. Has a brewery up in New Glarus. Now, I'm needin' some of his fine product down North Side Chicago way. Only his driver is...on an extended vacation, if you follow my meaning."

Jimmy nods a greeting. Joey and Gabe nod back. Joey says, "Yes, I think we'd be interested in that sort of thing."

Jimmy scrutinizes the two young men, looks at Bugs Moran for conformation, gets it from Bugs' broad smile. "Okay," he says. "Only one thing. You boys got a record?"

*   *   *

Federico Amarone was from the old country. He had brought the young grape vines with him, wrapped in cloth, protected them during the arduous sea journey from Veneto. Planted them and nourished them with his own hands. So too he had nourished his only daughter, using the fruits of his labor, so to speak, to provide her with a good home, good food and a love and respect for the land. Of all his accomplishments, it was she of whom he was the most proud.

He stood in his living room, heard the plaintive whimpering from his dog, Rufus, saw the wet, unreal lump on his davenport, looked at the faces of the two young men who stood there with him, and said in a voice which rose loudly but broke and cracked as he shook it out in gasps and spasms: "You sons of bitches! You God Damn sons of bitches! Out! Out! Get off my land!"

Rufus began to growl. Joey and Gabe backed out of the room, ran through the door and down the path toward the workers' camp.

In these earlier years the stock market crash of 1929 and the great drought of the 1930s, resulting in what would be called "The Dust Bowl", would devastate the agricultural economy all over the plains states, including Missouri. Workers that picked grapes and other fruit would leave the area to follow Route 66 to California along with "Okies" and "Arkies" and other migrants. Now, for Federico Amarone and other farmers of the central Missouri region, it was the calm before the storm...or lack of storms as the case would be. Joey and Gabe didn't head west, their ambitions were higher than most, high as their hopes to leave this nightmare behind. They headed up the highway toward Rolla.

Workers like Joey and Gabe were a dime a dozen and although Amarone had barely recognized the boys as two of his own, the sight of them standing over Cynthia's pathetic form was now a vivid and permanent element of his memory. Thus, when Sherriff Andrews interviewed him, he was able to describe them well enough for an all points bulletin to be issued. And it was issued. Police all over Pulaski County were on the alert for two scraggly characters, tall, thin, one with dark hair and one with light. And probably on the run. But the police cruiser that spotted them walking along Tear Drop Road had no need to run them down. They acquiesced quietly, even when Officer Callistino informed them that they were wanted for questioning in the rape and murder of a young girl named Cynthia Amarone.

*   *   *

On a cool Wisconsin afternoon in the spring of 1875, sixty-five year old Phineas Taylor Barnum sat on the front seat of his phaeton carriage, urging his favorite horse, Marengo, on with cheerful clucks and a light flapping of the reins. The high wheels of the phaeton, painted red and yellow with gilded hubs, easily traversed the rough dirt road between Barnum's bank in Kenosha and the headquarters in Delavan of P. T. Barnum's Grand Traveling Museum, Menagerie, Caravan & Hippodrome—in other words, his circus.

He was alone, preferring to transact business singly, especially business involving the exchange of paper money for gold. The carriage was stacked with supplies for his personal comfort, including a case of whiskey (had he recently given up being a teetotaler?), his leather suitcases and, cleverly concealed under the seat, a heavy wooden strong box bound with brass bands, secured with an enormous iron padlock. The key to the padlock hung suspended from a gold chain around his neck.

Barnum had ventured into circus ownership late in life, having essentially retired from his career in musical theater and museum exhibition of "curiosities." He was a master of entertainment and the exploitation of hoaxes and freaks, having introduced to the world the Feejee Mermaid, the Siamese twins, Chang and Eng, the twenty-five inch tall, General Tom Thumb, and the Swedish Nightingale, Jenny Lind. When coaxed out of retirement by his friend, William Coup, he brought with him his expertise with animals, large and small and his traveling freak show. He prided himself on his ability to misdirect the public's attention in order to put over some sensational, and impossible, stunt. Like a magician pulling a rabbit from a hat or sawing a woman in half, he was an expert trickster. He had, in fact, let it be known that this trip to the bank was along a very different route than the one he now traveled.

He wasn't suspicious, therefore, when he saw a man in the center of the road, apparently pinned beneath a fallen tree. He pulled up on Marengo's reins, halting the phaeton, and jumped down to investigate what he thought was a person in distress. He realized his mistake too late, when a blow on the back of his head sent him plummeting to the ground. Consciousness came only seconds later but he wisely lay still, seeking to avoid further misfortune at the hands of what was obviously some rogue. So it was that he heard the men talking, as they roughly yanked the chain from around his neck and he heard them call each other by name. Heard: "Pete," and "Lenny," and "Quickly, the carriage!" and "What about Barnum?" and "He'll be okay in a couple hours," and "Let's get the hell out of here!"

Pete and Lenny pounded tent stakes for Barnum's circus, an occupation that rewarded them little, neither financially nor spiritually. They had spent months planning this escapade, following Barnum on a previous trip and taking note of the change of route. The only flaw in their plan was that although they had the gold, they also had Marengo and the phaeton. To evade capture they decided to hide the gold and return to the circus.

"Boy, what a sucker!" said Lenny.

"Ha! There's one born every minute," said Pete.

They eased the carriage along the bank of Lake Comus, a small, creek fed lake on the outskirts of the circus town of Delavan. A sprawling ancient willow became the "X" marking the spot as they slipped the strong box into the muddy water. They left Marengo hitched to the phaeton by a small park in the center of town and, taking care not to be seen, returned to their rooms.

The next day, Barnum sat in his arm chair flanked by his friend and collaborator, William Coup and his paymaster, George Simons. A case of whiskey sat on the desk. Barnum, portly and balding, with the face of a smirking cherub, listened as Coup detailed his plans to ship the circus by rail, a strategy which would open up many distant markets. He had already related the tale of the robbery on the road and indicated his belief that the two miscreants were employees.

"George, I want you to ferret them out and eliminate them from our ranks. We can't have such vile scoundrels working for us. Their names are Pete and Lenny. That's all I know. Thank God they returned Marengo! Otherwise I would hunt them down and prosecute them to the fullest extent of the law! Try to rob me of my payroll, will they?"

Circus justice was sometimes more brutal than the letter of the law might allow. Several weeks later, the Barnum traveling menagerie was being loaded onto railroad cars. Elephants were used to push the heavy wheeled cages up wooden ramps and to load the massive center poles that would hold up the big top. Sometimes during the commotion and confusion of the loading there were unfortunate accidents. A wagon might break loose and roll over a man. A post or a roll of canvas might fall and crush a worker. An elephant might bolt and run down two men named Pete and Lenny.

*   *   *

Joey and Gabe stood before Judge Rupert Trumbull at the Pulaski County Court House in Waynesville, Missouri. Judge Trumbull was eighty-six years old and sharp as a carpet tack. He had drilled the boys over and over seeking any variation in their stories that would give him cause to throw their sorry butts into the county jail. He didn't like young boys who took underage girls swimming, especially when the underage girl turned up dead. However, the medical examiner had found no signs of sexual contact, testifying that the girl was, in fact, a virgin. Her bloated condition was consistent with the affects of multiple snake bite venom and no other bruises or abrasions were present on her body.

"Thus, while I cannot find evidence of wrongful death in the case of Cynthia Amarone, and the facts seem to coincide with the testimonies of one Gabriel Benning and one Joseph Venuto, I must rule, however, that extreme negligence exists in their having allowed the young girl to go swimming in snake infested waters. Therefore, I sentence the both of you to one year's probation, at which time, if there are no further incidents of this kind, you will be free to go your own way...which way, I would hope, will be somewhere out of Pulaski County," said the judge.

One year later, as their probation was approaching its conclusion, the boys found themselves working odd jobs in nearby Rolla. Everything was looking up. Except this year was 1929 and all hell was about to break loose. On February 14th, members of Bugs Moran's gang were rounded up by members of Al Capone's gang posing as police. Lucky for Bugs, he was running late that day. The men were ushered into a garage on North Clark Street and machine-gunned to death. This event would not affect the boys for many years to come, but it was one of the major battles in the most violent gang war in Chicago history, and one that would eventually be laid at their own feet with vivid brutalism.

On October 24th, the stock market crashed. Banks failed, People jumped out of windows. The Great Depression was right around the corner. In a way, Joey and Gabe were lucky: they already knew how to live poorly. They had nothing, they lost nothing. Life went on. They never saw Federico Amarone again who never forgave them for their role, however benign, in his daughter's death. Wary that the eyes of the law were constantly watching, they kept their noses clean...for a while.

*   *   *

In 1932, Joey and Gabe were working for Bugs Moran's Wisconsin bootlegger, Jimmy Murray, driving kegs of New Glarus beer to some of the "blind pig" speakeasies in Chicago. Al Capone was headed for the penitentiary in Atlanta. The Volstead Act, which had made the sale of alcohol illegal, would be repealed in another year, but the bootlegging business was still thriving. So too were the gang wars. Joey Venuto, the dark haired one, had grown a thin pencil mustache and was deemed attractive to the ladies. He had taken up with a girl calling herself Betty Barlow who worked at the John Barleycorn on Belden Avenue, a bar that had been boarded up in front, but could be entered through the Chinese laundry at the back of the building.

Joey and Gabe delivered kegs of New Glarus brew to the Chinese laundry on carts disguised as clothes hampers. The basement of the laundry connected with that of the speakeasy and on one such delivery Joey met Betty. She was a small woman with features that would be described as "cute." Pin curls and bobbed hair gave her a Clara Bow coquettishness and it didn't hurt that she could sing, even if her squeaky style was derivative of Helen Kane's "Boop-oop-a-doop". Joey was, of course, madly in love for the second time in his young life.

Gabe was cautious. He was reluctant to celebrate his friend's enchantment in the aftermath of their previous tragedy. For some, loss requires renewal; for others, retreat. The John Barleycorn could be a riotous venue on a Saturday night, so when Joey coerced him into catching Betty's last set Gabe was doubly beleaguered. Squeezed into a corner booth they strained to hear Betty's rendition of "I Wanna Be Loved By You" over the clamor and tumult of the Barleycorn's patrons. There was meager applause as Betty slid in beside Joey, her gig completed for the night. Betty greeted them with the one proclivity that most annoyed Gabe: she giggled.

"Can't we get out of here?" pleaded Gabe. The couple was billing and cooing, their fingers entwined. Ignored, Gabe gazed into the foamy glass of beer, seeing the froth and furry of river rapids; dire feeling rising within himself, like the effervescent bubbles before him, a dread, a foreboding of torment and tribulation. He swiveled the glass and foam cascaded to form rivulets on the table. As these emotive connections occurred in his mind's eye, a different image presented itself to his consciousness: one imbued with a devastating horror that trumped Gabe's dismal reverie. Standing before them was a man with a gun.

In the city that had invented drive-by shooting, where thugs eliminated each other at an alarming rate, where cops were on the take and the public, numb to the goings on, reveled in speakeasies, a little extra crime here and there was hardly noticeable.

The man was certainly a soldier in one of the gangs, North Side or South Side, take your pick. These were men whose calling in life was brutality and murder. It was just unfortunate that he was also Betty's husband and a mean, short tempered and possessive one at that. Betty didn't have much of a chance. Looking down the barrel of the .38 Special she only had time to say, "No, Bob..." and then the muzzle flash blinded and the sonic blast deafened and those left alive were covered in innocent blood.

There is a legend about a murdered woman who haunts the John Barleycorn. Perhaps it is true. There were now two young men who would be haunted by this second tragic death, a departed soul now dolefully conjoined to their personal histories. Joey held Betty's limp form and cried, "Oh no, God! Not again!" Gabe tried pulling him away, told him, "We have to go now!" Someone in the bar had tackled the gunman, wrestled him to the floor. Police were present. Turmoil ensued. It was not a good time to be a bootlegger in a speakeasy.

*　　*　　*

It is now 1934. Alcatraz prison opens and receives several notorious inmates including Alphonse Capone and Machine Gun Kelly. Other famous criminals aren't so lucky. Bonnie and Clyde, John Dillinger, Pretty Boy Floyd and Baby Face Nelson are killed by authorities. Prohibition has ended. Our heroes, Joey and Gabe, are out of a job. An old idea resurfaces: Barnum's gold is still out there somewhere. Wisconsin beckons them like a siren's song, sweet and tempting.

Lake Comus is so small, Joey and Gabe figure they could spit across it. It has been created by damming across Turtle Creek and functions as an alternate reservoir for the town of Delavan, Wisconsin. The circuses are all gone now and there aren't any elephants that need watering, so the lake is deserted when Joey and Gabe arrive, unload a canoe from the top of their borrowed roadster and start to circumnavigate Lake Comus.

"This won't take long," says Gabe.

"Look for an old willow," says Joey.

A spring breeze ripples the shallow lake. They can see sun fish and yellow bullhead stirring up mud near the bank. A lone Canadian goose honks overhead, perhaps commenting on the curious creatures below. They stop by a willow whose roots have been partially exposed as the shore has melted away through many years of rain and snow. They poke and probe the lake bottom, find a few small rocks, but nothing else. Methodically, they visit the next tree and the next, repeating their routine, carefully, like archeologists at a dig in Egypt, searching for the tomb of King Tutankhamen.

"Ya know," says Gabe, "we're looking for a tree that's at

least 60 years old, probably older."

"So how long do trees live, then?"

"Oh, plenty long, I guess. But it would be big. Real big. Do you see anything like that?"

Joey has to admit he doesn't see any likely candidates for the ancient willow tree of the story. Perhaps, he thinks, it is just a story after all. They continue looking and trolling the lake bottom until they have exhausted all the possibilities. They are pulling the canoe up onto the bank when suddenly, Gabe gets an inspiration.

"Wait a minute! We didn't see any really large trees, but...did we see any really large tree *stumps*?"

The canoe splashes back into the water, the boys following, jumping in and paddling yet once more around Lake Comus. They find it almost immediately. A tree stump nearly four feet in diameter. It looks as though it might have been a willow. No paddle probing this time, they jump into the shallows and reach into the mud. There is something there. Something large, rectangular and heavy. Struggling with its weight in the slippery lake bed, they manage to ease it onto the bank and start to scrape the mud off of it. It is, indeed, a strongbox. It is bound with brass straps and there is a large rusting padlock securing it. They hoop with delight. They have found Barnum's lost gold!

"Gabe," says Joey, "you and I's been through a lot together. We almost been in jail. We been shot at. We worked hard but we been poor as church mice. It looks like now's our time finally. You and me, buddy boy. This is our treasure now."

Gabe thinks about this. Somehow the promise of great riches doesn't excite him the way he thought it would. He sees where it could be just more trouble. What he really wants is to go back picking grapes, a simple life with no mysteries and no trauma. He's thinking he might just let Joey have all the gold. He might go to California. He looks at Joey, sees the lust in his eyes, the rising and falling of his breast like an overheated dog, the widening grin like that of a little boy with a new toy. He says, "It's all yours, Joey."

"Huh? What do ya mean? Never mind that. Where's a

rock? I can't wait."

Joey picks up the biggest rock he can find and dashes it against the rusted padlock. The lock crumbles. Joey's hands actually tremble as he raises the lid, pulls back the cloth that conceals the contents of the box. And stares in disbelief at a strongbox full of rocks.

THE FIRE NEXT TIME

Lord told Noah, build him an ark,
Build it out of a hickory bark.
Old ark a-movin', and the water start to climb,
God'll send a fire, not a flood next time.
                    —"Well, Well, Well," Gibson & Camp

Jason had wanted the telescope ever since he could remember. When he was a boy he had begged his father for one and received, one wonderful Christmas, a sleek metal cylinder with a hazy glob of bottle glass for a lens through which he could barely make out the coy expression on the face of the harvest moon. Now he was a young man of 21 years of age, earning his own living as a foreman at the lumber mill. He had saved and sent away to F. F. Arnold & Co. in Oak Park, Illinois, and the long heavy box had arrived by freight only yesterday looking very much like a miniature coffin with its brass handles and polished wood. This was no child's spyglass toy—no, this was a 3 inch, altazimuth-mounted Arnold's Educational Telescope with brass fitted wooden tripod: a reflective telescope suitable for amateur astronomers yet powerful enough to render visible the rings of Saturn on a cloudless night. It had cost three year's salary, over $350, plus $20 for the shipping, a small fortune for a young man in 1871.

Jason Howard lived in the small river town of Peshtigo, Wisconsin, located seven miles from the mouth of the Peshtigo River across the Green Bay from what some people called "the Thumb," and others called "the Door," a great peninsula protruding out into Lake Michigan like...well, like a sore thumb. Peshtigo was a village of approximately 2,000 people, making their living in one way or another from the stands of pine forests that surrounded the town. There was a large lumber mill at the harbor on the bay and several smaller ones, like the one Jason worked at, right in town. Some mills made window sashes, doors, shutters and the like. Jason's work place made decorative columns for porches, spandrels, gable ornaments and other bric-a-brac.

The town had sprawled across both banks of the river and was connected by a bridge and a railroad trestle. Jason lived on the west side on Emery Avenue in a modest boarding house run by a widow lady named Eleanor Sorensen. Mrs. Sorensen had lost her husband twelve years ago to a lumbering accident when a careless logger had failed to yell "timber" and a heavy Norway pine had split his cranium like a ripe melon. She was zealously religious and often pontificated about the Wrath of God and the coming of the Apocalypse, the genesis of which, she maintained in her scurrilous manner, was the pillage and plunder of nature by mankind—to whit: the lumber industry.

Jason took it with a grain of salt; she was, in her own way, a gentle soul in spite of her tirades. Often she would admonish him against working at the mill; someday the saw will slip, she said. Where Jason saw the products of the woodcutters as advancing his livelihood, Eleanor Sorensen saw the destruction of the old-growth forests as a defilement of God's plan: the desecration of Eden. What will she think, he wondered, when I set up my telescope in the backyard? Will she call it an intrusion into God's private sanctum? Ah well, she was a sweet old lady...bitter about the loss of her husband perhaps, but she meant well.

Jason could hardly wait to tell Brenda about the telescope. As today was Sunday he hurried to her parents' house on Ellis Avenue where she was staying, having come home between semesters from Wisconsin State Teachers' College. He had known Brenda since they had played in her sandbox, balanced precariously on the teeter-totter at the park, climbed the town's water tower in early adolescent derring-do, giggled together in merriment at the pompousness of the Episcopal priest while they held hands in a rear-most pew, and cried together when they parted—she to college, he to the mill.

Brenda was everything Jason was not. She was brassy and forward in social situations, especially if she thought the impression she was making might be scandalous or embarrassing. She always exhibited a visage of contrariness, a sly smirk or a ponderous pout, a mien of some secretive awareness that gave others, if they were perceptive enough, pause to wonder at her motives. But she could be the coquette, the charmer, the lighthearted fribbler that intrigued and enticed—this behavior was directed outward toward the anonymous world but never...never toward the one person who knew her, understood her, perhaps even loved her: her soul-mate, Jason.

What she liked about him was his timidity, his little-boy dependency, his unconditional adoration and willingness to please. This was not self-centered of her as she treasured their friendship. But her own diffidence, the insecurity which she covered up with an audacious persona, kept her fearful of loneliness—the one emotion she had no capacity to endure. Yet now she would hurt him, an inevitability she dreaded yet could not avoid. They never lied to each other; never withheld their inner-most thoughts and feelings. She had to tell him about Richard.

It had been a particularly dry summer. A drought plagued most of the Midwest. The wet lands and cedar swamps dried and even peat bogs lost their moisture. Needles dropped from fir trees and carpeted the forest floor in dull browns and reds. Angiosperms dropped their broad leaves even before autumn could come to emblazon the woods in polychrome splendor; the missing fall colors were much lamented by the denizens of Wisconsin. Small fires broke out here and there (which was not unusual), but this year the wisps of gray smoke sucked away whatever color remained leaving an ominous and joyless landscape behind.

The smoke worried Jason a little. He needed a clear sky for scouring the heavens tonight. He would ask Brenda to come over and be with him as he inaugurated his astronomical hobby. He had read in Popular Astronomy magazine about meteor showers that were predicted for this month as the earth moved through the coma field of Biela.

Biela was a comet that had caused much concern since its discovery in 1772, as its periodic returns came too close to the earth for comfort. The end of the world had been predicted with each return until 1852 when it was discovered that the comet had broken into two parts. Then it failed to show up for its 1865 performance. It was theorized that Biela had completely disintegrated and its fragments were due to descend to the earth as meteorites. These particles of space rock would be visible with the naked eye as they streaked through the night sky. Jason, in an enthusiastic burst of optimism, planned to search for the missing comet with his telescope.

"Come over tonight," he told Brenda. "I finally got it!"

She nodded, uncharacteristically silent. How could she tell this tender, fracturable boy that she was in love with someone else? His excitement over the new telescope was almost intoxicating. She fought off her angst and smiled widely. "How wonderful!" she said. That was all she said.

Eleanor Sorensen presided over the dinner table as usual. Jason and the other roomers at the boarding house were attentive as she said grace and then bid them all to enjoy her meager meal. John Sterling, a young man about Jason's age who worked at the Peshtigo foundry began talking about the present danger of fire to the community. Those idiot farmers were still in the habit of clearing land by setting fires, he complained. Didn't they realize the drought had created a tinder box out of the landscape? "There are fires smoldering deep in the peat bogs," added Stephen Anderson, another roomer who worked for the railroad. You could see the smoke rising like will o wisps and smell an acrid odor like rotted tobacco in an old man's pipe. He didn't allude to the sparks thrown off by trains passing through the dried forests although he was all too aware of it.

"And I looked, and behold a pale horse: and his name that sat on him was Death, and Hell followed with him," said Eleanor Sorensen, her voice cracking and just barely audible above the clinking of dishes and glassware. It was an abrupt but commonplace interruption by the matron of the household, yet everyone fell silent and turned toward her, knowing that the inevitable sermon could not be avoided.

"And the stars of heaven fell unto the earth, even as a fig tree casteth her untimely figs, when she is shaken of a mighty wind."

Now her voice had flattened and become louder, still at a conversational level, but rising as she talked. Jason fought an urge to grit his teeth.

"And when he had opened the seventh seal, there was silence in heaven about the space of half an hour. And the seven angels which had the seven trumpets prepared themselves to sound.

The first angel sounded, and there followed hail and fire mingled with blood, and they were cast upon the earth: and the third part of trees was burnt up, and all green grass was burnt up.

"And the second angel sounded, and as it were a great mountain burning with fire was cast into the sea: and the third part of the sea became blood..."

Eleanor Sorensen, her now trembling voice having reached a potentially window-shattering volume suddenly stopped her rant and slumped back in her chair, exhausted. The conversation picked up again, this time avoiding any mention of fire. After dinner Stephen Anderson walked with Jason down the hallway toward their rooms. He asked about the new telescope. Then he asked:

"These shooting stars in the night sky of late...could they fall to earth?"

"They are called meteors," answered Jason. When they fall to earth they are called meteorites. And yes, they fall quite often."

"Could they start fires when they hit?"

"Not really. They're always cold to the touch when people find them. I don't think it's ever been known that a meteorite caused a fire."

"That's good to know," said Anderson.

Jason unpacked the Arnold's Educational Telescope from its box and laid it carefully on the ground in Mrs. Sorensen's backyard. He assembled the tripod and mounted the pillar-and-claw platform to it. Upon this he hefted the forty-two inch focal length brass telescope with its three-inch achromatic lens and expertly tightened the mounting screws. Next to the box he had placed his books, Webb's *6 Celestial Objects for Common Telescopes*, Crossley, Gledhill, and Wilson's *Handbook of Double Stars*, and *Proctor's Star Atlas*. The telescope had come with two eyepieces, a four-lens eyepiece which inverted the image to its correct up-and-down position for terrestrial work, and an astronomical Huyghenian two-lens eyepiece with greater magnification for observing the sun, moon and the stars, albeit upside down. The later he now installed into the short tube protruding from the back of the telescope.

As he bent to line up the telescope with the North Star a pair of soft hands closed over his eyes. A voice said, "Guess who?"

"Um...Mrs. Sorensen? Mother? Oh...I can't guess. Who are you?"

"You brat!" said Brenda, jerking her hands away. "It's me...dummy!"

"Hi, Brenda. Meet my new 3 inch, altazimuth-mounted Arnold's Educational Telescope. Ain't she a beaut?"

"Oh, am I jealous! So this is your new sweetheart, huh?"

"Yep. Ready to have stars in your eyes?'

"It's been more like smoke gets in your eyes these days."

"Yes, but there's a bit of wind picking up and most of the haze is being blown away. Couldn't ask for a better night. Well...maybe I could, but I think it will do."

"What's a at...atlazmo mount?"

"Altazimuth. It's a mount with two independent perpendicular axes. The vertical one varies the azimuth or angle of elevation and the horizontal one..."

"Never mind. Jason? We need to talk. There's something I need to tell you. Something...oh...I've met somebody. Somebody I care for. Somebody I think I love."

Jason continued to fiddle with the focusing screw on the eyepiece. He wasn't good with extreme ups and downs of emotion: first the elation over the telescope and now.... He turned slowly, wiping his hands on his pants as if to rid himself of something vile that had slid through his fingers. He looked into her eyes, saw concern, saw sadness, saw in those dark blue irises a sort of reflection of his own shocked countenance. "I'm sorry, what did you say?"

"I've met a man named Richard. Met him...well, not exactly met. You see, he's my history teacher. We...oh, you don't want to know the details, do you? He's a dear person and cares for me. I...I didn't want to hurt you, but I thought you should know."

"Hurt me? Why should that hurt me?" said Jason miming as cavalier an attitude as possible. They stood studying each other with eyes darting back and forth between each other's lips and eyes, as if they were watching hummingbirds hovering in the wind before dead blossoms, unable to extract sweet nectar. A pair of shooting stars streaked across the sky, the beginnings of the Andromedids meteor shower, an event linked to Comet Biela's projected orbit. Jason's focus shifted to the heavens. "It's beginning," he said.

The meteor shower gradually increased from a few every five minutes or so to dozens every minute. Brenda and Jason were awe struck by the sight. Jason began scanning the sky, searching for the comet, but was unable to pick out any celestial body that could be either of the halves of Comet Biela. Some of the meteors had long phosphorescent tails which glowed even after they disappeared from sight. Some of the tails split up into particles with divergent paths of their own. They were now raining across the night sky at the rate of one every second and appearing to radiate from, Jason explained to Brenda, the constellation Cassiopeia which borders the constellation Andromeda which.... They were caused by the debris from the comet as it swung close to Jupiter; the "rain of fire" being larger particles entering the earth's atmosphere.

"If it's raining fire," said Brenda, "shouldn't we take cover?"

"How old is he?"

"Who? Richard? He's in his early thirties, I guess."

"He's an old man! How could you..."

"Oh, Jason. Please understand." But Jason was glued to his eyepiece now, fixating on his search for the lost comet.

"I do see something big up there. Here, have a look," he said motioning Brenda toward the telescope. She peered through the eyepiece.

"It's fuzzy," she said.

"Turn that knob. It will focus the eyepiece."

"Oh! What is that? Is that your comet?"

"I don't know. It's awfully close to be Biela, unless the theories that it would someday crash into the earth are true. Its orbit did come really close in...I think it was 1832."

"Oh...it's gone. I can't see anything."

"Smoke. The smoke is getting denser. You smell that? It's going to obscure the night sky so we won't be able to see anything. Oh, where is that wind when we need it?"

There was an old saying about being careful what you wished for. Wind! There was front to the west and south which was churning up a horrendous wind and it was about to reach Peshtigo.

Jason was perturbed. His night of star gazing was ruined—by smoke and by fractured romance. He started to pack up the telescope when the first flames fell from the sky to land on dry grass and roof tops.

"Oh my God!" Brenda shrieked. "It *is* raining fire!"

"It can't be. It's impossible. Quickly, into the house!"

But as they ran toward the boarding house the flames were spreading across its roof. Mrs. Sorensen burst from a doorway yelling, "The day of wrath is upon us! The Beast! The Beast shall hate the whore, and shall make her desolate and naked, and shall eat her flesh, and burn her with fire!" Brenda and Jason just stared at the woman who was waving her hands in the air frantically and repeating "The Beast! The Beast!"

Seeing that the boarding house was burning they had no recourse but to run—but which way? They instinctively ran toward the river. They still could hear Mrs. Sorensen wailing, "And whosoever is not found written in the book of life will be cast into the lake of fire...." People were running through the streets, blankets over their heads. Others were digging holes to crawl into like ostriches hiding their heads in the sand. Flames leaped up above the thick pine forests surrounding the town: a wall of fire hundreds of feet high was advancing, devouring everything in its path.

The fire had swept through the dried out swamp near the town of Sugar Bush and leaped onto a large barn filled with tons of hay which served to fuel its fury. The wind had reached cyclonic proportions and had blown the raging fire toward Peshtigo; then it had danced a whirling dervish of a dance that spat out tendrils of flame in all directions. Oconto and Pensaukee and Little Suamico to the south were threatened. Small towns as far north as Birch Creek would feel the intense heat. Menominee, Marinette and Menekaune would be devastated, And Peshtigo...Peshtigo would be incinerated, burned flat like a blackened prairie.

The firestorm would leap across Green Bay to drag its hot tongue cross the Door Peninsula, striking Williamsonville, Tobinsville and New Franken. What would become known as the Great Peshtigo Fire of October 8, 1871, would affect an area of 1,875 square miles, twice the size of Rhode Island—and the Wrath of God would not stop there. There were other fires that night: fire broke out across Lake Michigan in Manistee and Holland and Port Huron at the southern tip of Lake Huron. There were fires in Minnesota. In Wisconsin at least twelve communities would be totally destroyed and the death toll would be estimated between 1,200 and 2,500—it was impossible to get an accurate count of the charred bodies. The most famous of these simultaneous fires (although much smaller and less deadly than the Peshtigo fire) would be the one that turned a well known city into a cinder heap: the Great Chicago Fire. That one would be blamed on a cow.

God said fire comin' judgment day,
He said all mankind gonna pass away.
Brothers and sisters don't you know?
You're gonna reap just what you sow.

World's not waitin' for the Lord's command,
Buildin' a fire that'll sweep the land.
Thunder out of heaven, comin' Gabriel's call;
And the sea's gonna boil and the sky's gonna fall.
    —"Well, Well, Well," Gibson & Camp

By the time they reached the river it was filled with people; families clung together in the shallows, splashing water on their children's heads to keep their hair from bursting into flames. Animals had also sought shelter in the murky water. Pigs and oxen added their squeals to those of the humans. A horse ran up and down the shore, panicking, its back blistered and raw. The bridge had caught on fire and was collapsing; burning debris fell into the river and onto those few who were unlucky enough to have hidden under the bridge. Jason and Brenda eased into the cold water and moved to midstream where they could still touch bottom. Hot cinders rained down on the hapless, soggy multitude.

Suffocating and blinded by the smoke, many wandered aimlessly until they dropped in exhaustion before the infernal whirlwind. Women and children making for the river were trampled by horses and cattle. A pregnant woman struggled to the river's edge, her flesh singed and smoking, where she fell on the bank, gave birth to her child and then perished from the hot gases that had scorched her lungs. Someone grabbed the baby and plunged into the river with it.

At the Wooden Ware Factory an attempt was made to save the buildings. The village's fire engine had arrived and was wetting down the roofs but the tornado-like winds buffeted the buildings with super-heated air and flung the burning branches of trees against them: the fire crew was forced to give up. The engine was then moved to the factory's boarding house where a number of people, as many as 75, had taken refuge. By then the fire hose had melted. Flames struck the front of the building, then a mantle of fire surrounded the structure trapping the helpless men and women inside.

There had been little warning, other than the ominous smoke that had persisted in the air for the past weeks. Some of the residents of Pershtigo had packed their valuables in trunks in anticipation of a fire but now there was no time to drag these out of their burning dwellings. Showers of red-hot ingots fell like a hail storm and the heat was unbearable. A man frantically dug a hole to bury his valuables, sending his wife and children to run for the river.

He was overcome by heat and smoke and his family never saw him alive again.

Mrs. McDonnell of Lower Sugar Bush narrowly escaped death in the fire. She took herself and her family off to the plot of land they had recently plowed and there they dug a hole to bury themselves. The fire was so hot the dirt burned their faces and they nearly smothered, but they survived to tell their story to the newspapers. Mr. Abram Place in Upper Sugar Bush had the only house and barn that survived the fiery holocaust. Local Indians had told him there was going to be a great fire. He had had the presence of mind to clear a large area around his farm and filled every bucket and barrel he could find with water. When the fire did come, the Indians came back and soaked blankets and quilts with water which they placed on the roof. His buildings and live stock were saved. He opened his house later the next day to take in the suffering who had lost homes and family members.

Sister Adele Brise along with other nuns and some of the families in Robinsonville on the Door Peninsula rushed to the chapel where they cowered as flames surrounded the wooden building. Perhaps their prayers for salvation were answered as the chapel didn't burn—the congregation called it a miracle. Also in Door County, the town of Brussels was swept by flames which destroyed 180 houses leaving only five still standing. Nine lives were lost. At Birch Creek west of Menominee, all of that tiny town's six houses were burned and twelve lives were lost. In Menominee and Marinette people fled to the bay and jumped into the water. A steamer, the Union, took aboard over 300 women and children. Other women found their way to two other vessels anchored nearby. The male population of the villages spent the night fighting the fire.

Mary Drew was the wife of the lighthouse keeper at Green Island in the Green Bay. She and her husband, Samuel, had worked tirelessly keeping the lighthouse beacon burning to warn off ships from the rocks surrounding the island. With the drought, the lake had reached a dangerously low level and a thick smoke had rolled over the lake nearly obscuring the once bright beacon. Mary looked out the window that evening and saw an orange glow on the opposite shore. A strong wind blew out of the southwest carrying burning embers and ash which fell on the roofs of the outbuildings. Mary gathered her children together in the kitchen and began to pray, fearful that the End Times had begun. A schooner, the George Newman, was maneuvering off the island's shoals and failing to see the light ran aground, ripping a long gash along the hull below the waterline. The captain and crew made it safely to the island where Samuel and Mary saw to their needs. In the morning the surface of the lake was covered with ash and burned timber, the island's trees had burned and smoldering fires dotted the blackened landscape.

In Peshtigo the river teemed with people and animals. A few were so exhausted they floated down stream and drowned. One man had killed his three children rather than see them devoured by the fierce flames. Some committed suicide, so terrifying was the fire storm that roared like the biblical Beast of the Apocalypse. Brenda and Jason clung to each other, periodically ducking under the water to keep their heads wet. Still their skin turned red and felt as if hot coals had been pressed against their faces.

The wind subsided to a moderate gale, then dwindled to a light gust. A soft sprinkle of rain appeared, not enough to extinguish the flames but enough to give some sparse hope to the strife-ridden survivors in the stream. In only a few hours the fire storm had rolled, a tumultuous, turbulent cataract out of Hell, to flatten and obliterate Peshtigo and its inhabitants. Nothing was left: only cinders and ash, burning fagots that once were houses, and the charred and blackened bones that once were people who had lived and loved and labored and had not deserved this, whether it was the ultimate wrath of God, or nature's bizarre rain of fiery meteorites, or the result of some careless human spark that had grown into a rampaging, blazing catastrophe.

Three-hundred and twenty-five unidentifiable bodies like half-burnt sticks of wood were rolled into a mass grave. People wandered through soot and ash, looking for relatives or the remnants of their belongings. Brenda's mother and father had survived as had Jason's. But no one was unscathed. The wailing of mothers for lost children, of wives for lost husbands, of those who had lost entire families was a pitiful anthem played as a sad coda to a tragic symphony.

Jason returned to the boarding house—or to the place where the boarding house had once stood. As he shuffled through the cinders, the odor of burnt grass, burnt wood, burnt flesh hung in air that still stung the eyes. His foot struck something which he bent to pick up, then dropped quickly as it was still hot: a melted piece of metal, the remains of his telescope. Oh well, he thought. It's not the end of the world.

UP THE BIG RIVER

A chapter from the novel, *Once Upon a Gold Rush*. John Grosh, his brother, James, and his sister, Mary Jane traveled by wagon train from their home in Pine Creek Township, Illinois to Trinity County in Northern California in 1852 during the California gold rush. The novel, a work of historical fiction, chronicles their adventures. In this chapter, John is returning home on a steam-driven paddleboat on the Mississippi.

The Creole Belle, off Natchez, Friday, April 13th, 1860

John Grosh joined a group of first class passengers at the banquet table in the steamboat's salon. The table, draped with a lace cloth, was covered with large platters of various delicacies—pheasant, venison, fresh fish, oysters, nuts, fresh fruit—from which the passengers plucked tasty morsels at their leisure. Long-stemmed glasses of Champagne sat bubbling at the elbows of men and women in evening dress—John had worn his best suit but felt underdressed and uncomfortable.

A high vaulted ceiling ran the length of the salon. The luxurious space with its galleries and bars occupied nearly the entire Texas deck of the Creole Belle. Crystal chandeliers swayed and jingled from the motion of the boat. Along the sides of this expansive interior were the arched doorways of the staterooms. The decorative details of the salon imitated the Hall of Mirrors of the Palace of Versailles: glittery, and ostentatious; in fact, a great floor-to-ceiling mirror in an ornate gilded frame graced the far wall, visually doubling the length of the cavernous room.

John had sought help from Thomas Hardy, the first mate of the Witch of the Winds, in selecting a boat for passage up the Mississippi. Hardy showed him several packet steamers moored along the levee at New Orleans, and described what he knew of the captain of each. "The accommodations are of secondary concern," he pointed out, "to the skill of the pilots and crew of these flat-bottomed monstrosities."

Hardy had spent many years sailing the larger rivers in paddle wheelers and tugs before following his desire to take to the sea. Now he faced the prospect of having to leave the Witch of the Winds and seek employment again on some inglorious steamboat. Captain Stoughton, relieved at the outcome of the conflict with the Cuban slave-trader, had forgiven Hardy his transgression, but suggested that a parting of the ways would likely be the future for both captain and mate. Hardy was torn. He a felt loyalty to his captain and his ship, but was at odds with the despicable practice of running slaves, no matter how profitable it might be. He was still debating which path to take when John approached him asking for travel advice.

"Is your friend Tom Harris traveling with you?" Hardy asked John.

"Tom has decided to remain for a time in New Orleans," explained John. "He has met up with an abolitionist group involved in the Underground Railroad here in Louisiana."

"I've had a bit of experience along those lines, myself."

"They are quite active, it appears. There is an overland route they use to take runaway slaves north. Too bad they can't use the river."

"If there were some profit in it for the boat owners, it would be happening. Now if I had a boat..."

Seated at the table with John were a typical selection of

river travelers. A young married couple, Amy and David Albright, were on the return leg of their honeymoon cruise and headed home to Saint Louis, Missouri. Mr. William Yancey, a silversmith from Natchez, Mississippi, was visiting relatives in Memphis, Tennessee. A man named Jamie Raeburn, like John, was returning from the gold fields in California. He carried a heavy satchel with him, apparently containing the gold he had accumulated while out west. Ephraim and Agnes Brookville, an older couple, and obviously wealthy as could be seen by the extent of Mrs. Brookville's jewelry, were headed to Saint Paul, Minneapolis. Traveling with them was their daughter, Mrs. Margo Green and her two children, Alan and Roxanne. Mrs. Green and the children were presently in their stateroom. And lastly, Benjamin Hamilton was returning home to Chicago, bringing with him the bodies of his recently deceased wife and baby, who shared a plain wooden coffin now stored on the main deck.

Paddlewheel steamboats were constructed in layers, much like a wedding cake—which they often resembled. At the bottom, the hull was nothing more than a shallow barge, a design that enabled the boats to draught very little water and sometimes skim right over sand bars that would have stopped a boat with a keel. The hull supported the main deck which was open to the outside. Here cargo, usually bales of cotton weighing up to 450 pounds each, and wood or coal for the boilers were stored. Here too, passengers could ride at reduced rates. On this deck were the mighty engines with huge pistons pushed by steam from the boilers, linked to the paddle wheel by long rods.

The next deck was supported by pillars and held the boilers. Giant smokestacks rose up through the roof of this deck, their height crucial to preventing sparks from igniting the cotton bales. This roof was called the hurricane roof and served as a promenade area for the first class passengers. Perched on top of it was a structure called the Texas deck. A bit smaller in circumference, it housed the staterooms and the enormous salon. The staterooms each had two entrances, one into the salon and one out to the hurricane deck or sometimes, to a private balcony.

On the very top of the Texas deck was the pilot house. It

was a small cubicle with glass sides and was no less ornate that the rest of the boat. In it was the wheel from which the pilot steered the boat. The wheel was connected to the rudders by tiller-ropes. On this day, a Friday the thirteenth, Captain H. J. Blackwell was in the pilot house giving instructions to Eli Matson, his cub pilot. Matson was learning the river, a daunting task, as the serpentine waterway moved its banks every year and the resulting new sand bars and snags were an ever present danger.

Several of the crew were on the boiler deck, engaged in a game of dice. Jacob Stevens, having been elected as lookout, was watching out for the approach of the first officer when he saw a large brown rat scurrying across the deck. "A rat!" he cried, and the gamblers, thinking Stevens referred to a human rat, quickly exited the boiler deck. Stevens remained.

On the main deck there were thirty-five passengers including a German man and his wife and their seven children, four Black slaves belonging to one of the first class passengers, a pig merchant from Cincinnati, a squadron of soldiers being transferred to Saint Louis, and eight boys and girls from the Natchez Episcopal Church Children's Choir who were traveling with their choir master, Mr. Hebert Blackburn, to give a concert in Vicksburg.

In the engine room the chief engineer, Harold Craig, had turned in and left his assistant, George Dobbs in charge. Dobbs had inadvertently shut down the water to the boiler. Thinking he was increasing the flow he had turned the valve in the wrong direction. Tired from his ten-hour shift and a bit perturbed that the chief had gotten to turn in while he had to remain on watch, he leaned back in his wooden chair and closed his eyes.

The conversation at the banquet table in the salon was uninspiring. John tried to appear interested but Ephraim Brookville's droning on about horse racing was getting on his nerves. The young newly-weds, Amy and David Albright, only giggled and gave each other secret looks. Jamie Raeburn, the only person John might have had some common experience with, simply sat clutching his satchel, a dour expression on his face, and responded to John's inquiries about his gold mining adventures with a shrug.

John had just reached for the last oyster on the plate in front of him when someone observed that it was getting quite hot for an evening in April. Very hot and stuffy indeed! But then, the salon had no outside windows. Grasping at an excuse to detach himself from the boring company at the table, John announced he was going outside for some air. He exited the salon onto the hurricane roof at the stern of the boat.

The heat, coming from the boilers, now deficient of water, woke up the sleeping Dobbs. Realizing his mistake, he activated the force pumps to supply water to the boilers. That was his second mistake. The metal boilers were now super-heated. As the incoming water struck the white-hot metal a quantity of steam was produced that could not be contained: the boilers exploded.

One of the boilers was hurled intact toward the shore where it struck a willow tree, splintering it and setting it on fire. Another boiler was blown into fragments which descended from their flight through the night sky to land on a horse and dray, killing the driver and the horse instantly.

The snag-boat Goliath, commanded by Captain H. W. Dunbar, was one hundred yards up river from the Creole Belle. When Captain Dunbar heard the explosion he turned to look and saw flames leaping skyward from the ship. The air was filled with shards of wood, metal, and the bodies of human beings. The trees along the shore were draped with shredded bits of clothing, sheets and blankets, and dotted with chunks of compressed cotton from bales that had been torn apart. The next morning, severed limbs and unidentifiable body parts would be found among the debris.

The end of a piston cylinder on the main deck was blown off and a column of scalding water drenched the passengers. Some of those thus wounded tore at their clothing, ripping off flaps of skin that adhered to the cloth. Some jumped into the water to escape the agonizing pain and were drowned.

The pilot house was shattered by the impact of the explosion. Captain Blackwell, the pull chain from the ship's steam whistle still in his hand, was thrown fifty feet into the air and landed so hard against the hurricane roof he never regained consciousness. The cub pilot, Eli Matson was skewered by fragments of the wheel and blown off the boat into the water where he floated for a few minutes, his life's blood staining the muddy water scarlet, then he sank slowly beneath the surface.

The crew who had left the immediate area of their dice game were lucky to have avoided the cascading cloud of steam that enveloped Jacob Stevens. They ran around the deck, frantically trying to help victims who lay helpless or writhed in pain, screaming or weeping, or clutching at wounds that bled or blistered. Some were beyond help.

On the hurricane roof, John watched in horror as flames began to eat their way from the forward bulkhead along the deck toward where he stood. Passengers were hanging from the balusters, reluctant to drop the thirty feet into the river. Smoke was pouring up the stairways to the main deck indicating that fire blocked the way.

There were many people in the water below, hanging on to planks or cotton bales, mattresses, or anything that would float. Others struggled and slipped out of sight into the darkness of the river. Benjamin Hamilton was flailing about, his strength rapidly dwindling. He spotted an object floating several yards away and swam toward it. As he pulled himself up upon it he realized it was the coffin in which were his wife and infant son.

Amy and David Albright had reached the edge of the hurricane roof shortly after the explosion. David, in a panic, prepared to hurl himself into the river when Amy stopped him. "Wait for the lifeboat," she pleaded. "There are no lifeboats," he told his wife. "Help will come," she assured him. They then saw another passenger yank up a board from one of the benches and throw it overboard. He jumped after it and managed grab it before it floated away. David started working on removing boards from one of the other benches.

Captain Dunbar had turned the Goliath around and reached the burning Creole Belle in time to rescue some of those struggling in the water. He had two skiffs on board which he ordered lowered. The sailors from the Goliath rowed into the chaos and pulled people from planks often to discover they were already dead.

Jamie Raeburn was slowly slipping from the board to which he clung. The weight of his satchel caused the board to tilt. "Let go of the bag," shouted a sailor from the lifeboat that hurried toward Raeburn. "No! I can't!" he shouted back. Before the skiff could reach it, the board upended and Raeburn, unwilling to release his grip from the satchel, plunged into the Mississippi and was never seen again.

As the Creole Belle burned it sank lower into the river and rolled. Pieces of furniture were jettisoned from the salon through a hole in the wall and fell into the river. John saw his chance for survival when the long banquet table slid out of the hole, hung for a moment on the edge of the hurricane deck, and then tumbled over. He dove for it.

Flames burst from the two sides of the boat, flaring out and upward like giant hands that came together in a thunderous clap that propelled the combined inferno to an impossible height. Anyone still on the boat was incinerated. Then suddenly the boat sank and darkness returned to the river. Although most of the survivors had been pulled from the water by the crew of the Goliath, a few clinging to boards or cotton bales, had floated down river and out of sight. One by one they succumbed to fatigue or exposure or, disheartened by the loss of loved ones, simply gave up.

The banquet table had become an excellent raft for John, but unfortunately, not one he could steer. It was caught in the current and although he gave his best effort to paddling with his hands, he could not maneuver his raft toward the shore. In the darkness there was the danger of a collision with a steamboat coming up river. All he could do now was lay back and hope.

SOME INSTANCES OF HISTORY

In these stories there are threads of truth and threads of legend—legend that has become just as valid as truth in the remembrances of the tellers. For myself, I choose to believe. My characters are thus provided with a structure, an outline to follow that is often more fantastic than any author could invent. A few words, then, about what is (probably) truthful in these pages.

In the city park in downtown Delavan, Wisconsin, stands a monument of molded plastic depicting Romeo, the killer elephant. The marker on the front of the statue tells us that "Between 1847-1894, Delavan was home to 26 different circus companies. The Mabie Brothers U.S. Olympic Circus, then the largest in America, arrived here in 1847, to become the first circus to quarter in the territory of Wisconsin. Its famous rogue elephant, 'Romeo', stood 19½ feet high, weighed 10,500 pounds and is reproduced on this monument."

Most of what I've written about him here is true. Hauling Julliette out onto the frozen Delavan Lake and attempting to rescue Canada from falling through the bottom of a train car have been written about elsewhere and are at least as true as any of the old circus stories can be. Much of the lore comes from W. C. Cole's memoir, *Sawdust and Spangles* and from *Wisconsin Circus Lore* published in Madison, Wisconsin in 1937 as part of the Works Progress Administration's women's literary projects. I also used an excellent circus history source called "Olympians of the Sawdust Circle" from circushistory.org. Readers interested in our little town of Delavan might care to look for a copy of *History of Delavan* by W. Gordon Yadon.

Romeo wasn't lucky enough to have a kind handler like the fictional Tom Cavendish. He was frequently tortured in the name of training, a common practice among trainers who thought elephants were primarily stupid. He ended up with a broken tusk and a blinded eye. That he turned on humans, killing five people, is not surprising.

The spring, 2002 issue of Wisconsin History Magazine contains an article by Kimberly Louage entitled "The Bonds He Did Not Break: Harry Houdini and Wisconsin," in which she details events of Houdini's early years in Appleton, Milwaukee and Delavan. A more detailed account of the 12 year old runaway's adventures in Delavan appears in W. Gordon Yadon's "The Great Houdini's Delavan Connection." Then calling himself Harry White, Houdini was taken in by a local Delavan family, the Flintcrofts. There is a story about him walking 22 miles from Delavan to Beloit and back again to retrieve a letter mailed to him there. Did the strong circus presence in Delavan influence young Harry? Perhaps.

Were there giants in the earth? Several newspapers have reported the unearthing of skeletons of extra-human proportions over the years. The Phillips brothers, at Lake Lawn Hotel on Delavan Lake claimed to have found 18 skeletons that appeared to be ancient giants. Also, there were possibly as many as 200 Indian mounds on the property (Wisconsin abounds with mound-builder sites). Whether they contained the remains of very tall Indians or extraterrestrials is debatable. Skeptics of the existence of giants might be directed to look into the history of circus side shows of the nineteenth and early twentieth century where many people of high stature found employment. Oh yes, there were giants in the earth! Then too, there were Native American legends about a race of giants who lived on earth but were destroyed by the Great Spirit who felt they were too powerful.

The spiritualist camp at Wonewoc, Wisconsin is a real place with a colorful history. The Morris Pratt Institute at Whitewater, Wisconsin was originally designed as a temple and a school for Spiritualism long before it became a girl's dormitory. Was it haunted? There are those who suggest that it was. Spiritualism had an enormous following during the mid-nineteenth century. Key to the spiritualists' belief was the existence of mediums, mediators who could contact the nonliving. The popularity of this new religion did lead to the rise of many charlatans who used phony séances to scam the public but the majority of the seekers for the knowledge and confirmation of eternal life remained steadfast in their belief.

It wasn't until after 1870 that balloon ascensions caught on as circus events. There were independent balloon shows of course, but circuses avoided them for both practical and financial reasons. During the American Civil War, Thaddeus S. C. Lowe had introduced the military use of balloons and solved some of their logistical problems. After the Civil War ascensions grew in popularity and soon began to supplement the free circus parade as a major draw to bring in customers. The tragedy of the balloonist's death in our story is based on the real-life Rodney Palmer, an aerialist with the Buckley Roman Hippodrome and World Festival Circus who was to have ascended by balloon hanging by his feet from a trapeze over downtown Delavan in 1874. As he was ascending on that windy day, a guy wire became snagged and the balloon rolled over dragging him along the ground. He was smashed against the wall of the Park Hotel and later died of his injuries.

Eleazer Williams was born in Sault Saint Louis, Quebec in 1788. He was educated at Dartmouth College and soon joined the Episcopal Church, becoming a sort of missionary to the Oneida people of upstate New York. He moved with the Oneida to Green Bay, Wisconsin in 1821 where the tribe had joined with the Menominee and Winnebago peoples in obtaining a land grant. He married a Menominee woman named Madeleine Jourdain a year later. For a time he lived with and blended in with his "racial brothers," as he called them.

But by 1839 he began to claim that he was the Lost Dauphin, Louis XVII, who had been abducted from prison in France and had been brought to America and placed in the care of Thomas Williams who subsequently adopted him. He was, in fact, the heir to the throne of France, or so he said. His story is long and involved and much of it is explained in our short story. An interesting perspective on Eleazer Williams can be found in the writings of Franklin B. Hough who met with Williams in 1852. In 1937, MGM produced a short feature about Williams called "King Without a Crown." It premiered in Green Bay, Wisconsin.

There was a speakeasy called "The Sewer" in the

basement of the Lake Como Hotel. Jimmy Murray supplied it from his brewery in New Glarus. Bugs Moran, Baby Face Nelson and the Dillinger gang did hang out at the Lake Como Hotel in the 1930s. The original John Barleycorn on Belden Avenue in Chicago was a speakeasy during prohibition. It was accessed through the Chinese laundry. Barnum's gold? Well, that's debatable. The source...the only source for that story was an email sent to a local journalist in Walworth County. While adapting the tale for my story I had to change a few things to make it more credible. And where was the gold, you may ask? Why, in the whiskey case, of course.

In 1883, Ignatius Donnelly wrote the book, *Ragnarok: the Rain of Fire and Gravel*, in which he postulated that comets had been responsible for many catastrophic events during earth's early history. He suggested "that the present generation has passed through the gaseous prolongation of a comet's tail, and that hundreds of human beings lost their lives." This book led to speculation that the simultaneous fires of 1871 may have been caused by a fiery shower of meteorites, a theory that is debunked more often than not, yet still seems to explain the mystery of how huge tracts of land and cities separated by large distances could burst into flame *all at the same time.*

I hope to be forgiven for including the story about Riverview Park in a volume about Wisconsin. The link, for me at any rate, was the annual visit of my cousins from Superior and our trips into Chicago to the park. There was a real man named Popeye working there who could extrude his eyeballs from their sockets. And the parachute jump was as scary and dangerous as my character represents it. To me, Riverview Amusement Park and the State of Wisconsin existed in the same parallel universe: a surreal version of reality only visited in a half-dreamed state of mind.

ABOUT THE AUTHOR

Byron Grush was born and raised in Naperville, Illinois, just southwest of Chicago. He is a third generation native of that town. His grandfather, Alexander Grush, was a prominent citizen who served as mayor during the depression years of the early 1930s. Mayor Grush ran a soup kitchen and facilitated many WPA projects including the building of Naperville's Centennial Beach, a converted stone quarry that attracts many new residents. Byron's father, Byron Senior, was born above the meat market downtown in that city.

Grush studied art and design and taught at The Art Institute of Chicago, creating a course in film animation in the mid-seventies. He later became an Associate Professor at the College of Art at Northern Illinois University in Dekalb, Illinois, where he taught in the Electronic Media area. He is the author of a book on hand-drawn animation techniques entitled *The Shoestring Animator*. He and his wife moved to Santa Fe, New Mexico, in the 1990s, and opened an art gallery featuring Outsider and Visionary Art. They returned to the Midwest to retire in the small town of Delavan, Wisconsin, a place that reminds them of their roots. He is also the author of two historical fiction novels, *All The Way By Water*, and *Once Upon a Gold Rush*, both of which expand upon the probable history of his pioneer ancestors.

Made in the USA
San Bernardino, CA
30 September 2014